The Ghost People of the Everglades

D1520950

BARBARA TYNER HALL

PAGE PUBLISHING, INC.
Conneaut Lake, PA

First originally published by Page Publishing 2020

ISBN 978-1-64701-697-5 (pbk)
ISBN 978-1-66241-339-1 (hc)
ISBN 978-1-64701-698-2 (digital)

Printed in the United States of America

CONTENTS

SPECIAL THANKS AND ACKNOWLEDGMENT

To the Randal Daniels family for allowing me the opportunity to write and share the correct version of their story, and to Kent Daniels for telling me his side of the story for this book. As with any story that is well-publicized as much as this story has been, you have a lot of people that tell their side, but you also have people who claim the name the "Saltwater Cowboys" or the "Ghost People of the Everglades" to be theirs, but it never was.

I want to let people know that the Daniels family did not want to write this book, but they felt it was necessary, and there was no option with all of the many false truths out there about them as to what happened that needed to be corrected about their family and what they did for the town itself.

This book was written in the time period of 1974 through 1983.

Kent Daniels

PREFACE

The last frontier is no more, and drug-smuggling became big business in a small sleepy fishing village located in Everglades City, Florida, and an island called Chokoloskee. These small towns are located in southern Collier County and have a population of fewer than one thousand people.

The residents had traditionally made their living catching pompano, mullet, and stone crabs, as well as gigging frogs for some of the most popular restaurant chains in Miami.

When drugs flooded South Florida in the 1970s and 1980s, many of the local townspeople took to smuggling marijuana as their main source of income. The intertwined and dense mangroves of the Ten Thousand Islands that surround the area and the remote location provided a perfect environment for marijuana drug smuggling to bring and hide their bales in until they could deliver them ashore.

Only local fishermen that knew the backcountry of the Everglades and the complicated waterways of the area knew how to travel through the shallow waters and go through other passages unknown to anybody else. The local fishermen were sought after and hired to bring in large loads of marijuana from South and Central America as well as Jamaica.

When Operation Everglades One came down, it took a large majority of the men off the small islands and resulted in arrests or indictments of 149 people with more than five hundred thousand pounds of marijuana with an estimated value of more than 252 million dollars that were seized, along with cars, boats, and property with a value totaling more than five million dollars.

Drugs have ruined this town, the townspeople say at a local tavern that is a place the local fishermen frequent often. The fishermen are very distinctive with their looks. They have very hard bodies, huge arms, and most host scars left from the gnarly crabs that they so frequently fished. Most are hard-working, and their scruffy appearances and the white mid-calf rubber boots are a distinct giveaway as to what they do for a living.

But the crab men are not conveying anger or disgust for the men who haul the marijuana into the small fishing village; they are saying that drugs have destroyed Everglades City and Chokoloskee Island for the simple reason that the townspeople and the different crews that were running the marijuana into the area got caught.

This story is about one of the original families that were one of the first settlers in the area. This family was born into and knew the area like the backs of their hands. They became one of the largest crews available for hire in the Everglades. The Daniels crew was well-known to the area and well-sought-after for the hauling of the marijuana. This crew was dubbed the Saltwater Cowboy and the Ghost People of The Everglades and were wild and daring on the high seas as well as the complicated waterways of the Ten Thousand Islands. These boys could turn into the green door, which is a cluster of mangroves, and it would open up into another waterway just behind it.

This crew turning themselves in at the end of this decade of daring adventures served their time even though the crew was never caught with any drugs in their possession or in any of the many boats and airplanes that they owned and operated.

This is a story of an adventurous family that turned to illegal smuggling of marijuana after the laws changed and then took the majority of their livelihood away, making it harder from them to earn money for their families with all of the new fishing laws and regulations that were now in place inside of the backyards of the local townspeople they called Everglades National Park.

PROLOGUE

It was late afternoon, and Kent came by his parents' home to give them some disturbing news. When Kent entered the room, he found his parents troubled and upset. He sat down and proceeded to tell his parents of the news he had heard about a book that had been written and published on some of the events that the Daniels family was involved with during the period when they smuggled marijuana into the United States through the Ten Thousand Islands. Randal told Kent the book was not the only thing out there. Two of the people in the Daniels crew came out with documentaries. This book had things in it that the Daniels family had not given anyone permission to write. The man who wrote the book was never involved with the family crew or family and was not even from Everglades City. He was an outsider from one of the northern states. He even went so far as to use a name that was given to them by a media outlet in Miami. Joyce became so upset she had to exit the room.

Kent looked at his dad and said, "You know what this is about, Mom is so upset she had to walk outside."

Randal replied, "Yes, I do. It's the book."

The Daniels family felt as though the book was written on pure speculation. Randal became very angry about the book and the documentary.

Randal then explained to Kent there was not much they could do about this book being published or the airing of the documentary because most of what was in the book were of public record. "But let's make it clear the other writer did not have the permission to write about the Daniels family," Randal said. "I never wanted this to happen." He felt as though he and the family were being exploited, and the family felt they had served their time and did not want people to depict him as a hero or an outlaw.

"If you are going to tell the story about us, it has to be the truth, and it has to be your side of the story. The smuggling business was forced on us due to the economic situation from the new laws that were placed on the local people and the limits on what and how much fish we can catch and about what can happen inside and outside the national park. You have to say why we had no choice."

Randal then asked Kent that after this book came out, "I want you to make me two promises, one is that you will never write another book or documentary, and the other is that your mother has the right to proofread our version of our life's events. The last thing I ask is I don't want anyone but you, son, to mention my name in another book ever after this. Please end it."

Randal asked Kent to sit down, and he wanted to share with him about some personal stuff about the family and how all of this began. At that time, Randal told Kent how he met his mother and started the dynasty of the Randal Daniels family, and why they got in the business of marijuana smuggling, and how people took advantage of them, and how generous the family was to the small island in which they lived. He also wanted to make sure when their story was going to be told, it had to be accurate, and the whole story had to be shared.

He said since he was the head person and was charged so in the indictment, he had also asked the family not to do this, but a couple did, so there was no choice but to set the record straight.

The book that was written by people outside of the family and off the news stories and rumors had a lot of false allegations and innuendos that the family was so wrongly portrayed, and Randal felt it was very disheartening about the information in the other book.

The story is a story about Kent Daniels, Randal Daniels's oldest son, and the way he saw the family struggle and went from rags to riches and then riches back to rags. Please remember this is his recollection of the series of events that happened in the marijuana-haul-ing business that Kent himself and his family were involved deeply within.

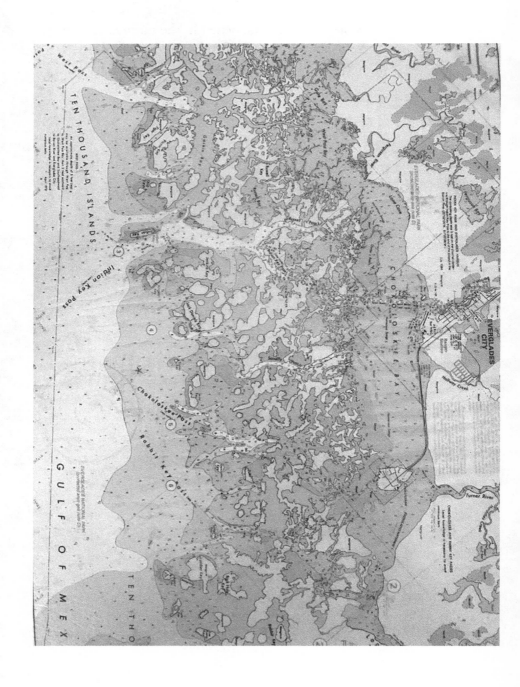

CHAPTER ONE

Chokoloskee Island

Florida's southwestern coast is made up of a group of mangrove keys known as the Ten Thousand Island. Chokoloskee Island and Everglades City are located eighty miles west of Miami just off Tamiami Trail on US 41 on State Road 29. The Everglades National Park is the western gateway to enter the park. Chokoloskee is one of the largest shell mound islands said to be built by the Calusa Indians or some other early settler.

In the early years of Chokoloskee, the only way to trade or communicate with the outside world was by sailboat to Key West. The first settlers only had a few choices on what they could to do to make a living. They hunted and fished. Fish were abundant at that time, and mullet was one of the fish of choice.

The story is about one of the first families who were one of the first settlers of the island called Chokoloskee, Florida, in the mid-1800s. This family has Indians in their bloodline; they lived like Indians and clan up like Indians. They were loyal, and they took care of each other first. With their olive-colored skin and dark hair and high cheekbones, it was thus making them very handsome and distinguishable from other people in the area.

These families lived off the land and fed their families utilizing illegal and legal hunting and fishing practices. Getting food from the land was no problem, especially for the local hunters. The waters were teeming with fish, and the Everglades themselves and the outer islands were teeming with wildlife like deer, alligators, and the white ibis wading birds locally known as the Chokoloskee chicken. They hunted, caught, and grew everything they ate; gardening was a big necessity for the people, but they also ate sea turtles and manatee. These known practices supported their families and made a decent living for the people of the area.

This way of life was handed down from generation to generation, and the skills were passed down from their elders. Living off the land was what the local people referred to when they were hunting and fishing in the area. Never took any more than what was needed to feed the clan or to survive.

Everglades was such a primitive place and did not have most of the modern-day conveniences, so the people lived in a harsh environment with very little money that could be earned to support their families. Their ways of survival were hard-labored in what they had to do to feed their families.

The island was an impoverished area, and the people were very poor and proud. Then in 1947, the government came in and started to regulate the area and designate it as a national park. The old ways of the settlers of the other islands became less and less. The people struggled every day to feed their families and survive. With the new laws, they were limited by our government as to what they could do on the land. Most people were forced from their land and homes without warnings, and then their homes were burned to the ground so they could not return to them. Everything they owned was lost.

The displaced people moved into Chokoloskee Island and The Everglades City area and now call it home. Now the national park has become ever stricter with their regulations, leaving virtually no way for the local people to survive. Living in the last frontier was challenging from day to day. It took strong men and women to survive in this harsh environment, and many didn't.

People in this area had no cars, homes, or ways to continue to make a living for their families, with no money to relocate to other cities, leaving these families devastated and with no option but to turn to illegal practices. Like moonshine during prohibition to alligator poaching, and now came the marijuana smuggling into this distinctive area. Some of the descendants still live in the area to date, and they still struggle with the new regulations that seem to change every few years.

CHAPTER TWO

The Family

The story started with the love that Randal had for his wife, Joyce, and the events that led to the establishment of the Daniels family, better known as the Ghost People of the Everglades, and as Kent listened closely, Randal told him just how the family started with the perfect love story.

One day, Joyce caught the eye of a young man named Randal while they were attending church. Randal was the type of guy who had a reputation of dating other women for a short time and then moving on. Joyce knew of the reputation, but she was still infatuated with him but was never allowed to be alone with him.

One night they went double-dating with another couple, and they went parking at a place most kids hung out, which was on Dan House Road; so towards the end of the evening, they drove down and parked. It was a beautiful clear night with the stars sparkling like glitter in the sky. Randal had been driving, so they parked, and the other couple had stepped out to stretch their legs and walk around, so Randal and Joyce remained in the car; this way they could talk and get to know each other a little better, and after a few minutes, he reached over and kissed her on the lips and instantly she knew this one was real. When they finally broke free, Randal looked at Joyce and said, "What in the hell did you just do to me."

Seconds ticked by while she stared at him, trying to figure out what had just happened. In her head, she was screaming *Oh God is this for real* as she was jumping with glee. When everyone returned to the car, Randal drove slowly, savoring every minute he had left with her that evening. They drove straight to the house. No one was talking.

She stammered to say good night as he went around and opened the car door for her. He then walked her to the front door of her home and said good night. As Randal drove off, he realized he gave her his heart, and he left that night with hers. The new beginning of a beautiful relationship and marriage grew.

The men from this area were known to be hard, gruff, and hard-working, but when they loved, they loved deeply and with their whole heart, and it was forever. Nobody could have ever asked for anything better.

Randal and Joyce have five kids: two boys and three girls. Their marriage flourished with deep, devoted love and respect. The family, like most families in the area, fell on hard financial times. Randal was doing anything he could do to feed his family and survive. He relied on his older children to help out wherever they could, especially the boys. Randal and his family struggled every day, not realizing that a new industry and job opportunity were just on the horizon.

Once the marijuana-smuggling entered the area, this newfound financial freedom was hard to turn away from, and it was the beginning of the new dynasty, and the Daniels family entered into a new and exciting era in the next chapters of their life.

Everglades City in southern Collier County was a small town with less than one thousand people in the population. The residents had traditionally made their living catching pompano, mullet, and stone crabs, and gigging frogs, and this little town was one of the largest suppliers to many restaurant chains in the Miami area, as well as others in the state.

When drugs flooded South Florida in the 1970s and 1980s, many of the residents turned to marijuana smuggling. The money was more than they had ever seen in their whole life. It was very tempting and luring. This ideology was a no-brainer when you were looking at the poverty surrounding them and with kids and wife to feed. It was a done deal.

The dense mangrove islands that surrounded the area was the perfect remote location and provided an unbelievable camouflaged environment for the best routes to bring the marijuana bales ashore without being detected.

Local fishermen who knew the backcountry and knew how to maneuver through the shallow waterways were well-sought-after and were hired to smuggle marijuana from Jamaica, South, and Central America.

*****

Today, a fourteen-year-old boy named Kent Daniels lived and was raised in the area. The grandson of Albert and Lavinia Daniels and the son of Randal and Joyce Daniels.

Albert and Lavinia had six sons: Wade, Dewayne, Randal, Darryl, Sherald, and Craig. The Daniels clan were men of men, straightforward and to the point. They said what they meant and meant what they said. This is the foundation of the Daniels Crew better known as the Sat Water Cowboys.

On one evening, Randal was feeling pretty rough with a good case of the flu, so he had no choice but to give the task of earning money for the family to his fourteen-year-old son named Kent. Kent was told he had to catch 400 pounds of mullet that night, which were a local fish in these waters. To get the money, the family needed to survive.

Kent entered a tight, narrow waterway moving through the dark waters and passageway of Green Turtle Creek and coming out on the other side, where it opened up into Gaston Bay. A boat approached him, and he slowed down, and he saw it was Phillip, one of his dad's cousins, so he stopped, and Phillip said to him, "I need your boat."

Kent responded, "I kind of need my boat too so I can make a living."

Phillip said, "If you come with me, you will make a living."

Kent said, "You don't understand. I have to have 400 pounds of fish at the fish house in the morning, or my dad will be mad at me."

Phillip said, "You would have the 400 pounds of fish in the morning I will make sure of it, I need the boat, just come with me."

At that point, Kent realized he was playing with a double-edged sword. Kent was speaking to an elder, and being southern, he never disrespected an elder. So if he didn't do what he asked of him, he would be in trouble, and then if he didn't have the fish that he needed in the morning, he would be in trouble with his dad, so Kent did what he was asked to do.

Phillip handed him a ski mask that covered his face. He then told him to go to a specific location and wait until he saw a light blink, and then he was to head to where the light was blinking. He was told not to speak, not to take the mask off, and do as they told him to do. He would get his instructions, and they would tell him where and what to do next.

When he came up to the boat, and they got finished loading it, he was told to go up sand fly pass right in the mouth of the bay stay in the islands and wait until he saw another light blink, and then he was to ease his way across the bay to the bridge, being careful not to make any noise. When he got to the bridge, two people got on his boat, and started throwing these large bundles off the boat, and walked them up the side of the bridge to a waiting van.

The drugs were offloaded into the vans, and then he was told to take the boat to the center of the bay and bail it with water and clean out any residue that might be behind.

Kent went back to fishing, and it was now around midnight, and he knew he had to catch the fish that he needed for that evening. He caught 200 pounds of fish and took them to the local fish house to be sold. Whenever he offloaded the fish at the dock and weighed it up, the person collecting and weighing the fish asked him if he wanted him to add the fish to the 400 pounds of fish he had already brought in that evening. He let him know that Phillip had already done what he told him he was going to do so he wouldn't get in trouble with the family. He replied to just add it to his ticket for tomorrow.

Kent lived at home with his parents, and two days later, the house phone rang, Joyce answered it and said, "Kent, Phillip would like to speak to you."

He got on the phone, and Phillip asked him if he would come and see him at his house. So Kent went to Everglades City that evening to visit Phillip at his home. When he arrived, Kent knocked on the door.

Phillip yelled, "Come on in."

As Kent entered the room, Phillip tossed a small brown paper bag to him, the kind that was made to place a can of beer inside. He asked him, "What is this?"

He replied, "Your pay for the other night."

Kent looked at him and said, "I didn't know I was getting paid, and how much is there?"

Phillip replied, "Fifteen thousand."

Kent yelled, "Fifteen thousand dollars!"

Phillip looked at Kent and said, "I have a job tomorrow night, do you want to be on it."

He was standing there shaking his head no, but before he could stop himself, his mouth said, "Yes."

On his way back home with the money stashed in his pocket. He went straight to his bedroom. Sitting on the side of the bed with the money in his hand knowing he couldn't tell Mom, Dad, or anyone else about the money. Not knowing where he was going to hide it. His mother was like most women in the area. She would change the sheets and flip the mattress once a week, and she would dust everything in the room and move the furniture around if she needed to, and she would find it. Looking around the room as to where to hide it, he was looking at the dresser where he kept his clothes. Taking one of the bottom drawers out, the little piece of wood separated the drawer from the floor, so he took his pocket knife out and pried the wood up, and he put the money on the floor between the drawer and the floor. He put the drawer back and thought to himself that no one would ever find it.

About five jobs later, he came walking into the house, and Randal was sitting at the kitchen table with a bottle of vodka and a can of Coke sitting in front of him. He grabbed the bottle of vodka, turned it up, and took a big gulp out of the bottle and slammed it down on the table. He turned and looked at him and asked in a deep cold voice with his eyes cutting right through him and said, "Who in the hell did you kill?"

Before Kent could respond, he picked up a can of Coke and chased the vodka down.

Kent replied, "I didn't kill anybody, what in the hell is wrong with you."

Taking another big gulp from the bottle of vodka and another hit of Coke, he asked him, "Then what bank did you rob. If you will tell me, son, I will do my best to help you."

Kent replied, "I didn't rob a bank, nor have I killed anyone. What in the hell are you talking about."

Not remembering the money at this point, his poor mother stepped around the corner with this brown grocery bag and walked over to the kitchen and dumped the money on the table and asked, "Where did this money come from?"

Mom was in the process of doing her spring cleaning, and she had found his stash of money. At this point, Kent felt he had a lot of explaining to do.

Kent turned and looked at his dad and said, "I have been hauling pot."

Randal stood up from the table and looked at Kent and, with his left hand, pointed at the floor, shaking it up and down.

"Your goddamn mother has been hauling pots and pans around this house for years and has never made this kind of goddamn money."

"I have been hauling marijuana,"

Daddy said, "What the hell is marriage-ja-wanna?"

Then his mother replied, "Randal, he is on that dope that these young kids are on, and he is going to go to prison or die."

Not knowing how true her words would become, he walked over to a chair at the kitchen table and pulled a chair out and sat down, looked at his dad, and asked him to sit. Kent took the bottle of Coke and took a big drink out of it and said, "Daddy, this is what

21

is going on." He explained how much money he would make a night and how the job was done.

Daddy looked at him and said, "Can I get in it?"

"No, I am making enough for all of us," Kent replied.

"No, I was told there were only two ways of getting out of this, death or prison, and it is not if you get caught, it is when you get caught."

A couple of days later, he had been gone and came back to the house and noticed that Daddy wasn't there, and he asked his mother.

"Where is Dad?"

She replied, "He had gone grouper fishing with a man named Totch."

Totch made radio contact to get someone in his crew to get ahold of Randal Daniels and get him out to the boat and help them out. A couple of hours later, Kent found out from rumors around town that Totch had a heart attack on the boat, bringing a load in. The boat was carrying fifteen thousand pounds of pot on it. They needed someone who knew the water around Fort Pierce. Which Randal did from his younger days of mackerel and king fishing. Randal was flown to Fort Pierce and picked up by a smaller boat and then taken out to the big boat offshore, and Randal did not hesitate and brought the boat straight into the dock in bright daylight with the boat loaded with the fifteen thousand pounds still on board and saved the load.

The Daniels crew were some of the best people around. They would help each other out in a time of need, even if it meant risking their own life.

After the job was over and Totch received medical attention he needed, Totch then returned home and was talking with some people who had visited him when he returned from the hospital, and he then proceeded to tell them what Randal had done for him and the crew and how he had the biggest set of brass balls he had ever seen on any man in his life; he was fearless.

CHAPTER THREE

The Start

Craig and Mike were heading out mullet fishing on a dark starry clear night on a well boat. The boat was called a well boat because of the motor sets in the front section of the boat, midway to the bow. The net was always released off the back of the boat, which was called the net table.

The guys were in great form and eager to get their catch done and get back home for the night. Craig and Mike were heading through Turtle Key on their way to Rabbit Key grasses to fish when their boat started bumping and running into stuff in the water. After feeling three or four big bumps on the side of the boat, Craig looked at Mike and said, "What the hell is going on?"

"I have no idea," Mike said.

Craig and Mike turned their headlights on and looked over the side of the boat. They saw these things floating in the water, and Mike asked, "What is that?"

"Damned if I know," Craig said.

"Grab one, and let's check it out."

Reaching for his pocketknife, he cut the burlap sack open. He looked inside and said, "Mike, it looks like marijuana."

Mike reached in and grabbed a handful and smelled it and said, "*It* is."

Craig looked at Mike and said, "Let's grab a couple and get it in the woods and come back for it in the morning."

After they hid the stuff in the woods, they returned to their favorite fishing grounds. Mike looked at Craig and said, "Do you realize how much money we have in those two bales?"

"Yes, I do. It is totaling about one hundred fifty thousand dollars right now at three hundred dollars a pound."

In the early morning, they set off to the area they found the stuff in, and to their surprise, no more bales were floating. The three they had were probably all there was. Craig saw the boat when they were fishing. Craig looked at Mike and said, "This was a job, and they must have lost a few bales off the boat."

"I think I know where they hid their stash."

"I think we can go get some more."

"If we play our cards right."

As he moved through the waters and with Craig knowing the water as well as he did, they came across exactly where the drugs were stashed and hidden in the woods.

Craig said, "I told you it would be here."

Craig and Mike went to the stash with their hands raised saying, "Don't shoot, I just want a job."

"You know who I am and where I live."

"I am going to take ten bales and tell the big man to come and see me."

"I just want another Job."

Mike came in and told Craig, "I want to sell the two, I don't want any part of the ten, you do what you need to do with the other."

Craig and Mike loaded the stuff up and went back to Craig's house. Craig grabbed a shower and got something to eat when a knock came to the door. Craig answered the door, and it was Phillip, the big man.

Phillip said, "I think you have something that belongs to me."

Phillip then said, "What do you think we should do about it."

Craig said, "I would like to have another job."

Phillip replied, "I think we can work something out. I have a job coming up in about two nights, and I will come by and tell you when and where."

Craig told Phillip where he had hidden the bales and let him know how to get them. Phillip left to retrieve his goods.

CHAPTER FOUR

Craig's Job

Two nights later, Phillip came by and told Craig they needed to be at the bridge around ten o'clock. "I'll have someone come by and pick you up and give you the instructions. Do not talk to anyone about this." As expected, the car showed up right on time and dropped Craig off at the Chokoloskee Bridge. Craig was nervous as they waited for the first boat to arrive, out of six, around eleven o'clock at night. Two guys would jump on the boat, and the other guys would form a human line, passing the bales of marijuana one by one to the top of the road until the vans were completely loaded. After they finished and the last van left, they dropped Craig at his house and called it a night.

After two days had gone by, Craig got a telephone call from Phillip asking him to come to his house. A brown sack that contained his pay was tossed at him just like they had done his younger brother.

Phillip came to Craig and said, "The job we had for tonight has been messed up again. The big boat has run aground just inshore of Turkey Key."

Craig looked at Phillip and told him, "I can go get that load."

"Craig, we think the law is around it."

"Yes, but you don't know that for sure."

"No, we don't."

"Are you sure, Craig?"

"We can't leave the guys on the boat and let them get busted."

Craig asked Phillip, "How much is on the boat."

Phillip responded, "It is ten thousand pounds."

"And we are going to need five boats."

"Two thousand pounds per boat."

"Can you get a crew and boats together?"

"Consider it done and tell them, guys, I want to meet up at Duck Rock just before dark. I am going to go down and make sure everything is okay and check it out before the boats get there. If there is any problem and the law is there, I will stop the boats right there and turn them around. If not, we will get the job done."

Craig met the boats at duck rock. He told the boys, "I haven't seen any law around or any activity in any way, so let's go on down to the big boat and get this done and don't mess around get it and get out." Craig said, "When you get your boat loaded, head up Chattam Bend. We are going to put it up there in the woods by the old Watsons place and put it by the creek. Once the heat from all the law enforcement agencies cools down, we will come back and move it out."

Once the weight got off the big boat, it started to float with the tides. He put another man on board and told him to take it offshore and clean it up, making sure all of the residue were off the deck, and anchor it offshore but make sure it was deep enough water, so it didn't go aground again.

When Craig offloaded the stuff at Chattam, he headed offshore to pick up the crew guy who was on the big boat. About the time Craig got to the boat offshore, a helicopter hovered over the boat, and when Craig was approaching, he turned, and at the same time, a marine patrol boat came up and turned his spotlight on them with the blue lights on.

He asked, "What you are guys up to."

Craig replied that he found the boat drifting around. "I was scared it was going to run aground, so I put one of my guys on it to take it offshore and anchor it off out here so it would not tear the boat up."

The guy said, "Are you sure that is what you guys are doing."

Craig responded, "Of course, do you think I am stupid. I ran up here with both my lights on, the boats running lights, and anchor lights. If I was doing anything stupid, do you think I would have had my lights on so you can see me?"

The officer said, "You have a point there. Where is the owner of the boat?"

"I guess he went fishing and the boat got loose from the anchor and drifted inshore."

Most people in those days would tow their smaller boats behind the big boat so they could fish and put their catch on ice. It wasn't uncommon for the fisherman to stay down on the water for two or three nights while fishing. With no small boat attached to the larger boat, it looked like the owner was just out casting his fishing net.

Years later, sitting around talking about old times, Craig was bragging and told Kent that he was the first in the family to get into the hauling of the marijuana, and Kent thought he was the first to have gotten into this industry. Craig was like a brother to Kent, and Kent looked up to him, but unbeknown to Kent, Craig was one of the guys unloading the boat and taking it up to the van; and unknown to Craig, Kent was one of the captains on the boat with the mask on his face. The crew was so closed-mouth about the newfound industry that these two had entered into, they did the same job and didn't even know it.

CHAPTER FIVE

The Godfather of Marijuana

The Godfather of Marijuana, Buddy, came to town. Buddy was the big boss, being the first man ever to bring the marijuana into South Florida, and he came to talk to Craig.

"Craig, I want to thank you for the job you saved, we would have lost the load. I would like you to get your crew together and work for us. Can you get the family together and work for me through Totch and Phillip? Nobody knows the waters and the backcountry better than the Daniels men, and I need that kind of knowledge on my side. But you are going to run the crew."

Craig finished his conversation with Buddy, and they agreed to all the terms, and then he set off to recruit the Daniels clan for their future endeavors.

Craig knew he had to contact everyone in the family. He also knew he could not pull these jobs off without them. Randal had fallen on hard times economically and was looking for a job to make money for his family. Craig was on his way down to Darryl's house. Darryl had a boat that he was having a problem with leaking. Craig opened a sack of money and told Darryl to take what he needed to fix his boat.

Darryl was shocked, and his eyes were huge, but he said nothing and went to pick up the phone and Craig said, "Please don't do that. You're calling the cops."

"I'm not," Darryl responded.

When he picked up the phone, he called Randal and said, "You better come over here now." Randal arrived about twenty minutes later.

"What in the goddamn hell is going on."

Randal spoke with a large booming voice when he was a little excited. Randal looked at the money and said, "Goddamn."

Craig explained, "I am giving you a chance to get in the business with me. Here, I will pay you ten thousand dollars a night for two nights."

Darryl said no right away.

Craig then told Randal to go to the bag of money and take as much as he needed for his family.

"I don't want the money, I want a goddamn job," Randal replied.

And then Darryl finally came around and said, "Okay then, if he is in, then put me in it as well."

Craig said, "Okay, get your boats ready and gassed up, and I will let you know where and when the job will take place."

A day later, Craig received instructions for the job. Randal and Darryl left Craig's house, getting everything prepared for the job later on that night. After a few minutes, they realized they needed extra help, so they contacted Paul. With him being reluctant and kicking the brothers off his property at first. Then he finally agreed to be a part of this job that night.

It was a warm night with calm winds, and the sea was slick as glass, and the stars so bright they would light up the sky. It was a beautiful sight to gaze up at the peaceful and calming purple clouds dancing across the black sky.

But then reality set in when the anxiety started to get going. "We have a job to do, and once you start the boat up, you know what could happen." The boys knew when they left the dock that this could be the last time the crew ever came home. In silence, they prayed for a safe return and asked God for a good and peaceful trip with a bounty big enough to take care of all of the families on these boats that the crew needed to provide for their families. But they had no idea what this trip would entail or what they would be facing. After they would arrive at the destination, the boats would gather and go silent. The anticipation hit hard as the radio squelched, and contact was made with the mother boat, and that was when the small boats anticipated what was going to happen next. They could hear the gurgling noise of the mother boat coming in. There was a distinct sound the exhaust of a boat made when it was loaded. The exhaust of the mother boat was half underwater and half above water. It sounded like a purr gurgling in the middle of the water. As soon as the guys heard that all-too-familiar sound, they ran straight for the mother boat. All the guys jumped off the small boats, except the captains, and got on the big boat and pitched in to offload the marijuana on to the smaller boats as fast as they possibly could.

Once every boat was loaded, and the crewmen were back on board, everyone followed the lead boat to a certain destination. Craig looked at Randal and said, "You take the lead, and we will follow you in." The destination was Chokoloskee Island, at a place called Snook Alley. No homes were there at the time. It was all grass. They had brought vans down to the end of the alley just before the waterfront and just before the guys had shown up. As they loaded one van, it would pull out, then the next and the next until they were all was gone. The vans headed east to the Homestead area to their confirmed meeting spot. They would then collect the partial payment for the job and then return home.

The group always held back a portion of the marijuana to make sure they got paid for doing the job. They held more than what the job was worth to guarantee payment. Once the crew was paid, they would send the last of the marijuana over that they had held for the final transaction.

After a tedious and pressure-filled job, the guys decided to take a few days off to blow off some steam. Randal and Joyce had just recently purchased a home outside of Nashville, Tennessee. The house was a haven for the family. A place where they could go and get away from it all. Randal and Joyce also felt the need to purchase another home for safety reasons and a place they could stay for long periods. Randal realized that some of the jobs were not always easy, and some of them were downright dirty. Some of the bigger people involved in this industry were vicious, and Randal felt that any time, they were going to encounter trouble. He would send Joyce and the family to stay at home in Tennessee until the job finished, and Randal would join her. Randal and Joyce came from an area in Florida that was never prone to violence or any other type of criminal activity until this new industry entered the small island of Chokoloskee and Everglades City.

Joyce and Randal went on vacation, so this left the house in Tennessee for Kent to enjoy and use. Upon arrival, Kent had some friends up there that he had already met. One of the people he met was called Charlie Daniels. Through Charlie, Kent was told about and taken to a local tavern called the Stage Coach Lounge off Highway 40. The place was perfect a hideaway, where they could unwind and kick back in a good atmosphere that Kent enjoyed and frequented often. The owner of the bar and Kent became close friends. Kent being from Florida speaking with a true Southern drawl. The accent was appealing to many that had encountered him in the Nashville area.

The bar itself was set to the left-hand side of the parking lot. It had a strip mall in an L-shape on the right. A very large establishment. The numerous times that Kent had encountered the club, he noticed that several of the Country and Western legends frequented the lounge as well. The way that Kent had met these people was because they noticed a slow Southern accent that he spoke with. They would get together and talk about stories of their lives, and the one thing that appealed to them was where he was from and the tales of the Everglades, and Kent was a great storyteller, some true and some exaggerated. One of the things they seemed to have caught the interest was the stories of the airboats, how they could run on dry land and go through water, and how they used them for pleasure and hunting.

One day they were sitting and talking about the airboat, and they asked if Kent could have the airboat brought up. Kent then went to the bar owner and asked if he could use the phone. Kent placed the call asking his cousin to bring the airboat to Tennessee. After speaking with Gary, they decided that he would bring the airboat up. Kent then proceeded to tell him where he could find the keys to his truck and to get it loaded and get it up here. Gary took the favor very seriously and drove all night and part of the next day to get the airboat to Tennessee where Kent was.

When Gary arrived, he lay down and went to bed after driving all night. Kent had told everyone else that he would meet them at the lounge when it arrived. Kent went on over to the lounge with the airboat, and when he walked in, he asked the owner where everyone was.

And the owner replied, "Let me make a phone call, and they should be here shortly."

Kent then told the owner the airboat was outside.

The owner responded, "Airboat."

Kent said, "Yes, an airboat."

Yes, this was a ten-and-a-half-foot full-deck with a TA 180 Lee Colum, which meant it was aircraft worthy. The airboat was built by one of the best boat builders from the Florida Everglades area by the name of Wayne Sage.

After about thirty to forty minutes, everyone started showing up. They met outside in the parking lot and were talking about the airboat, and there were about ten people gathering around to start. One of the guys looked at Kent and said, "Let us take her off the trailer and go for a ride." Kent was game for anything but was not familiar with the icy conditions of the parking lot and the area in which they were about to use for the ride on the airboat. Kent was very familiar with using the airboat in warm weather conditions with water and grass, but there was no water or sawgrass anywhere in sight, and this was the first time Kent had attempted icy weather conditions with the airboat and in his life in general.

Kent stepped into the driver's seat, and another gentleman got in the passenger seat behind him, and he placed his hand on his shoulder and said in a deep baritone voice, "Let's do this."

Kent reached down and turned the key and started the airboat motor, and with his hand on the throttle, keeping in mind there were no neutral or breaks on an airboat. The only way you could stop the boat was by spinning the boat around and powering it out and letting off the gas and shutting the engine off, and it would stop moving in water or grass.

Kent gave a little throttle to get the boat moving. He was going down the parking lot towards the other side, and getting down to the other end of the parking lot. He now realized this was not going to be fun. The boat reacted differently on ice then it did on water. He spun the boat around, and on the way back where they had started from, and in between two cars, a medium-sized dog weighing about thirty pounds ran out right in front of the airboat. Kent was turning the rudders to dodge the dog, and he ran right over the top of him. Kent was turning around and looking behind him to make sure the dog was okay, which caused the boat to go into an unnecessary slide that he couldn't maneuver the boat out of.

Hitting the first car and bouncing off it and then hitting another car and bouncing off it, he was finally back in the part of the parking lot they had already come down and was getting the boat straightened out and moving the boat back into the original area of the parking lot, cutting the engine off, and the boat was still moving sideways Kent decided that he needed to start the motor back up and get control of the boat. The noise of the motor was loud like an airplane, and it just so happened to catch the attention of a passing local state trooper. Kent was now easing the boat back up and trying to regain control of the airboat, and the state trooper stepped out from between the two cars holding his hands up as he yelled, "Stop!"

Kent then cut the motor off again, and needless to say, the damn boat didn't stop, and it then ran over the top of the state trooper. Now please understand the boat was a flat-bottom boat and did not hurt the dog or the trooper. Starting the motor back up so he could spin the boat around and check on the state trooper's well-being, by the look on his face, you could tell he was not happy with the airboat or the man driving it. The boat was still drifting toward the trooper, and the trooper was still a little stunned. He reached out and grabbed the front of the boat by the grass rake; he looked up at Kent, and he didn't know if he was going to shoot him or arrest him. He then looked at Kent with white knuckles and said, "Where in the hell are you from, boy."

Kent replied, "Deep South Florida."

And then at that point, Kent was told to "Get the goddamn boat back on the trailer" and "Get that goddamn boat back to Florida because that damn boat sure as hell does not belong in Tennessee."

And about the time the trooper finished speaking, a larger-than-life gentleman, who was nicknamed the Man in Black, was in the back of the airboat in the passenger seat and was stepping off the boat by the state trooper and said, "Hi, my name is Johnny."

Everyone started laughing, and by this time, they had drawn a pretty good crowd of people.

After that state trooper cooled down and he decided no one was hurt, they loaded the boat on the trailer with the promise that he would not take it back down off the trailer until he reached Florida. Then they walked back inside and had a drink and believe it or not, and just by the grace of God, no tickets were issued, and the dog was out walking around where all of the excitement had taken place.

Kent then told the state trooper, "If you ever get down to Florida, look me up, I would love to take you out in the Everglades and give you a proper ride, but as you guys could see, and believe me when I say this, my airboat boat does not work well on ice."

After two days and partying all night, Kent and Gary decided to head back to Florida and go home. Gary was probably a little more sober then Kent. So Gary had the task of driving, and he decided they were going to go by Ruby Falls in Chattanooga, Tennessee.

Heading up the side of the damn mountain and Kent not liking heights, he looked at Gary and said, "What the hell are you doing?"

Gary replied, "I want to go to Ruby Falls." Looking at all of the animated carvings on the walls and heading to the lover's peak. There was a swinging bridge you had to cross over when Gary grabbed the side of the bridge and started shaking it and said, "Don't worry, you will be fine, Kent."

And just as Kent crossed about halfway through the bridge, Gary shook the bridge with Kent on it. Kent dropped to his knees and scooted and crawled off the bridge and refused to go back across it. After they got Kent calmed down, they then proceeded to get in the elevator and go down in the caverns of Ruby Falls. They decided to turn the lights off to show every one of how dark it was in the cavern. When the lights came on, Kent had his hands around this lady's waist. When the lights came back on, he apologized to the lady, but she could tell he was really scared. The lady started singing as part of the tour, and she had a beautiful voice, and it was customary to tip the people who had entertained the visitors.

Kent had asked the lady why she had not recorded her music when the lady told him she could not afford it. This area of Tennessee was very poor economically. Kent then proceeded to ask her how much it cost to do the recording, and she told him. Let's say Christmas came early for this young woman, and there was enough money given to her as a tip so she could get her music recorded.

CHAPTER SIX

Purchasing New Boats

After three or four jobs and after everyone made some money, the guys decided to go out and buy newer and faster boats. The well boat was twenty-four feet in length and eight feet wide and made of a fiberglass hull, making them run forty miles an hour at top speed and with a 235 Johnson engine that you could get out on top of the water and plane. With four thousand pounds of additional weight, this boat would still run about twenty-five to thirty miles an hour. The boat was also self-bailing, so that meant that the bales stayed dry. This boat was designed and built by a guy named Walter from Marathon Key. The order was placed, and the five custom boats were bought and purchased. As soon as the boats were ready, somebody had to get them and bring them back to Everglades City.

The engines were purchased, and the five boats were rigged with all sorts of much-needed components, and the motors were mounted on each of them to ready them for the next job. These boats were costing above seven thousand dollars each, which with one job, it more than paid for the boats and then some.

Little did the family know that with the new boat purchase, it brought attention to them. People are human, and they love to talk. Seeing new boats come in really got the town buzzing and going around with all the latest rumors about who had purchased the boats and what they were going to be used for. Let's just say this might be some attention the crew may not have wanted.

Craig went to Randal and Darryl and said, "Guys, we have a big job coming in. This job is thirty thousand pounds, we are going to need seven boats, we have five, and now we need two more."

Randal said, "Craig gets Odalph and Kelvin. They have a couple of larger well boats that we could use. Tell Odalph to bring Brett with him as his crew and tell Kelvin to bring Mike for his. These boats should carry approximately five thousand pounds each".

Craig said, "You guys get the boats ready for this job, and we have to be ready to ride."

Little did they know that when the five new well boats came into town, it drew the heat down on them. They now had the county deputies and the park rangers watching every move the Daniels crew was making.

The boats were at the dock and fueled up. When the guys hit the dock and took control of the command of their boat, their stomachs would begin to knot up, and their nerves would take control of each of them. They would start to dry-heave. The not knowing about what was going to happen would get the best of them. The guys never knew the unknown, like if they were going to be busted, jumped, or shot at, or even make it back home alive safe. This would continue until the guys got across the bay. But only when they could fire up their engines and take off across the dark black waters would these feelings start to subside and finally go away. The guys did not carry any guns, the law did. As they moved into open waters and once they opened the motors up and got going, they could speed up the boat and let the wind start blowing in their faces, and that was when their stomachs would finally settle down, and that was when they knew they were free to do what they needed to get done.

Everyone on the boat had anxiety and felt the pressure of the job. Especially the captains; they always felt responsible for the crew returning safely. It was a lifestyle you were living and playing cat and mouse games with, your life as well as the other people on the boat. But in reality, it was no game; you could be shot dead right out on the water and could never to be seen again.

The job happened, and everything was going smooth. Down by little Pavilion, they all met up offshore to make sure everything was cool, and they arrived as undetectable as possible, and there was no law around. Everybody entered the area in different ways to make sure that no one saw them, and if so, not everyone would be spotted, and the rest of the boats could make a clean getaway.

It was nine o'clock, and it was dark, and there was a light northwest wind on a cloudy, wet drizzling night. They sat there waiting on a VHF radio call. The call would come in a coded form. It would say something to the effect of, *I am skipping pompano*. Craig would come on and say, "Let her go." This would mean the boat was close, and the coast was clear. If the law was around and the law was hot after them, Craig would come on and would have said, "The sharks are eating my net up." That would mean "be careful and get the hell out of there."

Everybody's ready, and they all ran over to the big boat named *The Sally-Ann*. She was sixty feet long and had thirty thousand pounds of marijuana bales sitting on her deck. The crew would jump into action as soon as they pulled up alongside her and start to unload *The Sally Ann*, making sure everyone got the same amount and making sure no boat was overloaded.

As they got to the end of the offloading, John saw several caged roosters, and he asked, "What are we going to do with these damned roosters?

The guy looked at John and said, "We bring them over to sell them. They're fighting roosters." The man set a pen with a rooster in it on the deck not knowing the door was open on the cage. The rooster ran out and started running around the deck of the boat, John tried to catch him. When he did, the rooster spurred him in the leg. Let's say this was one hell of a battle between John and the rooster. The rooster battled his last fight, and John won that particular fight and then left this job with a battle scar and a hurt leg.

Now all the small boats were loaded and headed in with Randal and Odolfs in the lead, with everyone following them. On the way in, the crew was still laughing and carrying on about the rooster and John. Now they arrived at Joe Camp Key. Off in the distance, about a half of mile or so away from their destination, the crew noticed the blue lights flashing off in a distance. They had spotted *The Sally Ann*.

The hearts of the crew sunk, and they knew it was game time. It was a known fact that when you got jumped by any of the law, it was every man for himself and to never throw the bales overboard unless it was necessary.

Everybody ran in different directions. The blue lights light up the dark night in all different directions, and the helicopters were up in the air and were trying to shine spotlights on any of them to show which direction they were heading in.

Kent was a crewman with Craig on this job. Everyone separated, and they ran to rabbit key grasses known for its shallow waters. Craig and Kent were talking back and forth.

"What do you want to do?"

Craig responded, "I just want away from the law."

Kent responded, "We have secret creek or auger hole, pick one."

Craig said, "Which is the closest and the fastest to hide in."

"Secret Creek," Kent replied.

As he turned and looked behind them, Kent could see the blue lights flashing. Behind that, toward the water they just came from, was a helicopter with the spotlight still hovering over *The Sally Ann*. He could tell the blue lights were now directly behind them and getting closer and closing in.

"Craig they are gaining on us, but we only need about ten more minutes."

Please, Lord, just give me ten minutes more so I can keep everyone safe and get us home tonight, Kent prayed.

Kent replied to Craig, "And you have to know the area because the water is very shallow and muddy with a lot of oyster bars."

Craig's boat was a fish hawk, which was a little narrower and drew about six inches more water than the others.

Craig looked at Kent and said, "You know the area?"

Kent replied, "Yes, I do."

Craig said, "Then you take us through it."

Kent took the helm, and he brought the boat through secret creek to the first bay. By this time, the blue light was just a couple of hundred yards behind them now. Kent knew if he made one wrong turn, he and Craig would be on their way to jail. He knew ahead of them there were two oyster bars, and the top of the bars would be out of the water. Between the two bars, the boat would have just about fifteen-foot clearance to make it through the two oyster bars and pass right on by. The deepest part of the space between them was only about a foot and a half deep—just enough water to get them through.

He looked at Craig and said, "Hold on, I have to make a sharp left and sharp right. I have to go between these two bars so we can get away." They came through to the other side good with the blue lights still on them, but the law did not see him make the left and then the right turn, and the park ranger went straight ahead and grounded his boat right on top of the oyster bar. This was happening on a fallen tide, which could be very bad and could leave him aground for six hours or so to sit and deal with the swamp angles (mosquitoes). This would give them enough time to make a clean getaway.

Craig and Kent made it over to Rutter bar pass. He slowed the boat down and turned the motor off and told Craig, "Let's sit here and listen for a minute."

They couldn't hear anything, no noise of any kind. Which was a good sign. He then looked at Craig and asked, "Do you want to put this in the woods?"

Craig replied, "No, let's take it in."

They eased the boat across Chokoloskee Bay towards Chokoloskee Island. Craig grabbed the mike to the radio and said, "I have a bright night, and it is a full moon." Meaning "we are coming in with the load, be ready."

The radio came back on and answered, "The stars are bright, and it's a beautiful night," meaning everything was good, so they eased over to where the vans were parked and got it offloaded as quickly as they could.

Craig asked, "Has anybody else been in?"

"No," they replied.

"Where is everybody else?"

"We didn't know if we were going to be busted, and they had already caught *The Sally Ann*."

"So we split."

At this point, Craig said, "Kent take the boat and wash it out and take it to the dock." The golden rule was at any time if you got jumped, you never went back out to take a chance of scaring your guys, and you could not take a chance of hitting one of your boat head-on or causing more confusion than was unnecessary. The rule was a known rule throughout all the crews. The marijuana haulers made it for safety, and everybody abided.

CHAPTER SEVEN

Fame and Wealth

With the fame and wealth of the new industry in the area, the local people prided themselves on helping the community out. Marijuana money and other monies donated built the community center for the local people and the skating rink, and the park was designed and built for the children. Churches received large anonymous donations large enough to feed and clothe all the children and families in the area of Everglades City and Chokoloskee Island. The town had no fire station and was in dire need of new equipment for a new one. All the townspeople gathered and physically built the fire station, just showing the tight niche community these two small islands were. All of this was possible by the newfound industry of Everglades City and Chokoloskee Island that had entered into their neck of the woods.

The people were proud, and they gave from their hearts. All donations were anonymous, and no one ever talked about who did it, nor did they ever boast about what had been given.

As for the local families involved in this trade, they donated money to a few churches and the school as well. The money was used to rebuild the buildings and to operate the ministries in this small-town area. The men may have smuggled marijuana, but they never lost their faith in their Christian ways. They always worshiped the Lord and Savior and relied on their Christian views to bring them home safe and sound. This may sound a little conflicted, but you have to remember the Christian ways were here long before the marijuana and drugs.

With newfound money came a lot of added incentives and pressure to maintain a new lifestyle. New cars, trucks, homes planes, boats, and old homes were being remodeled with the proceeds of this found enterprise that helped this area so rapidly.

These people educated themselves with the outside world by traveling and doing things that they could not afford to do prior and seeing what was beyond the little island they had grown so comfortable in and proud to call home.

With the newfound wealth also created newfound problems. The Daniels crew never hauled anything but marijuana, and they wanted to make that clear, but other drugs entered into the area as well. Cocaine, Quaaludes, acid, and PCP just to name a few. With the new drugs came unexpected grief. Some workingmen would no longer work, and the kids became party animals and out of control. Parents could not or would not control them. Money was spent carelessly like it was nothing, and a fountain was overflowing with the money for the rest of their lives. With that kind of money, the kids and the parents became bored and had no idea what to do with themselves next. The newest and the fastest cars, boats, and planes were bought and given to the young crowd to entertain themselves. The next big thing to be introduced would be a new and different type of drug. With this new edge, and the combination of the two, more lives were lost than could have ever been expected at young ages. Young men and women were incarcerated for long periods during their youth. Most of the innocent youth were lost during that decade. Parents buried their children, and children buried their parents; this was the ultimate price to pay.

The townspeople felt as though the drugs destroyed Everglades City for the simple reason that the townspeople who were running the drugs got caught.

This is not a malicious statement. What they are referring to is the people were poor then became extremely rich, which boosted the economy locally, and local businesses soared to new heights and levels that had never been seen before.

CHAPTER EIGHT

Date Night

Craig and Kent had a date in Naples that evening, and they needed a car to get to it. They wanted to borrow Joyce's car. Randal had just bought Joyce a brand-new Delta 88. The first time she had ever owned a brand-new car in her life. She only had the car for a week.

Kent told Craig, "I am sure we can borrow the car. You talk to Daddy, and I'll talk to Mama."

They walked upstairs, and Kent went to their mom and dad's room and asked if they could use the car because they had dates. Randal said, "It's not my car. You have to ask your mama."

Kent promised his mom that he would have the car cleaned up and full of gas, and they promised not to hurt it in any way and to promise the world, and it would be back by morning. Keep in mind this was Joyce's first new car, and she was so proud of it.

So Craig and Kent went to Naples, got that car detailed and shining it like a new penny. From there, they took it over and had the oil changed in it and filled it with fuel. They went and picked up the girlfriends and went and got something to eat. Played around with the girls a little bit, but the girls had to be home by ten o'clock that evening. The boys were in town, and not wanting to waste the time they had there, they headed to the back-door lounge. Having a couple of drinks in the bar, and with the band playing and everything going good, Kent lost track of Craig. When he turned and looked at some crowd with a lot of noise coming from an area of the bar, he saw Craig dancing on the tables. Kent laughing and shaking his head, he sat and watched. Craig finally got off the table, and he had another drink, and Kent could sense that there was a fistfight on the horizon.

The Daniels boys were known for fighting. They said if there was alcohol involved and no one wanted to fight with them, they would fight among themselves. Kent never sat with his back toward the door. This night for some reason, he chose to do so. When Craig was dancing on the table, Craig had knocked over and spilled someone's drink.

The guy came up to Craig and said, "Hey, you are going to buy me a drink."

Craig said, "If you are telling me, I am going to do it, and you're not going to get it. But if you ask me, I will do it for you."

The guys were known not to talk a lot, but they were also known to let their hands do their talking for them. The guy wanting the drink reached up and put his finger in Craig's chest. Craig was fast with his hands, and he was a fast mover. Let's say within five minutes, Craig had already beat the man's eyes shut, and Kent had to get him off the man.

Most of the time, when you were in a bar, and one fight broke out, there was always someone who thought they were bigger and better than you, and they liked to jump in the fight, so the shit just got real and hit the fan.

When the fight finally broke up, they walked back over to the bar and had a drink. He looked at Craig and said, "We should get Mama's car back to her. It is already 1:00 AM, and she will be looking for us."

They got in the car and headed home. They decided to pull into McDonald's and get something to eat and drink for the ride home. They were leaving McDonald's when they looked up and saw one of their friends walking on the side of the road, so they picked him up and gave him a ride. On the way home, Craig was lying against the passenger seat window, and Steve was lying across the back seat, and Kent was driving. Just before they got to the Port of the Islands, which was a resort that was located just about halfway to the Everglades, Kent looked up and saw something ahead of them in the middle of the road.

Kent yelled, "Oh shit!"

Craig jumped up and looked, and there was a twelve- or thirteen-foot alligator walking across the road. Which stood almost two feet tall, the alligator went from the white line from the shoulder of the road to the yellow line in the middle of the road. That was one big alligator, and he knew if Kent hit it, the car was in trouble. Well, there was no stopping, and Kent hit the alligator. The impact of the collision was so horrific that Craig's head hit the roof of the car and indented the car roof with a perfect impression of his head, and poor Steve was slung off his seat and put in the floorboard. When the car stopped, they had gone off the road. The car finally came to a complete stop, and upon inspection of the car, the boys came to a conclusion pretty quickly that the car was drivable, but it was totaled. They all got out of the car and were looking at the damage. When Kent looked up and saw what they had hit he said, "We can't leave the alligator in the middle of the road for someone else to hit." So they all three got together and pulled the big alligator out of the middle of the road and over to the side, and they left it there, keeping it out of the way of other passersby.

Babying the car along and driving it very cautiously to the house, finally, they made it home. The next morning, they had to tell their mom and dad what had happened. Randal did not believe them. Calling a wrecker to have it towed was a chore, but it was one that they had better do if they didn't want their mama on their backs after hours passing by waiting to see if the car could be fixed or not at all.

Randal asked, "What you hit?"

Kent replied, "An alligator."

Then Randal replied, "I think you hit a guard rail and went over it."

"No, I didn't, Daddy," Kent said.

It took three weeks and four thousand dollars to fix Mama's car. Their dad still didn't believe the story about the alligator. Randal went out into the area to look for the alligator carcass but never found him.

Randal told Kent, "Why don't you just tell me the truth."

Kent and Craig drove trucks, and back then, they only had one seat, and four people needed to be in the truck for the date. That was why they borrowed the car in the first place. I can tell you now, it was going to be a very long time before they ever asked to borrow the car again.

The next evening, Kent went to Naples, and when he was driving back, he stopped at the Port of the Islands and had a drink. When he came into the bar, he realized his dad was sitting at the end of the bar with another couple of guys. About the time, Kent had gotten a drink, and Randal started on him about the car again. He couldn't leave it alone because he thought the boys had lied. He then looked at him and said, "Son, you hit the guard rail, just tell me."

"No, I hit an alligator. It was at least twelve feet."

The guy sitting on the other side of Randal said, "Excuse me, I didn't mean to overhear your conversation. Did you say you hit an alligator right up here with a car?"

Kent replied, "Yes, I did."

The man asked, "What kind of car was it?"

Kent replied, "It was a Delta 88."

The man then said, "I am a game warden, and we had been trying to figure out what happened to the alligator. We thought a truck had hit it. I bet that car of yours is torn up."

"Yes, four thousand dollars' worth of damage."

Randal said, "You did tell me the truth. It was an alligator?"

The man replied, "Not just an alligator, the damn thing was fourteen foot long, and they had to get a trailer to haul him out on."

Randal turned and looked at Kent and said, "I guess by God, you did hit an alligator. I guess by God, you did tell me the truth."

CHAPTER NINE

Lost for Three Days and Nights

Dwain called up the Oyster Bar Restaurant and got Randal on the phone.

Randal asked Dewain, "How are things going?"

"Not good at all," Dwaine replied. The block company is going under, and I don't know how I am going to pay my bills."

Randal said to him, "Do you have enough money to get down here, Dwain?"

Dwain replied, "I can scrape up enough money to get there."

Randal then told him to get there, and he would give him a couple of thousand dollars.

Dwain replied, "Where you are going to get that kind of money?"

Randal said harshly, "It doesn't make a damned bit of difference where it comes from, just get here."

Dwain said, "I would be there first thing in the morning."

Randal said, "I would have some Chokoloskee chicken fried up for you."

Kent and Joe were put in an airplane and flown to Marathon Key. Where Eddie met them at the airport and picked them up. Eddie had a twenty-four-foot Robalo with twin 200-horsepower engines. The job they were going to do was in Shark River.

Dwain and Randal had to sit down and talk.

Dwain asked, "Where you are getting all this money?"

"The family is in the marijuana smuggling business."

Dwain replied, "You know this is illegal, and you all could go to jail."

He looked at Dwain and said, "We have a job tonight, do you want to be on it? It pays fifteen thousand dollars."

"Yes, I want to be on it."

"Be ready just before dark, we will come and get you."

Everyone was heading to Shark River. It was fifty miles one way. This area of the Ten Thousand Islands was the furthermost they had ever traveled for a job. Other jobs were also coming into the area for other crews, so they felt like it was too hot to use the same area, so they moved their trip further south.

They all met up at Shark River just after dark. Shark River was a river that ran north to US 41, and it had two different sections that branched off and went into two different directions. Joe and Kent left from Eddie's house in Marathon Key. It was about an hour for them from Marathon.

They all got there about the same time. When Kent arrived, he realized that Bobby, his younger brother, was on the job as a crew hand on one of the boats. The boat was already waiting on them at Shark River, and the big boat's name was *The Lady Karen*, with about twenty thousand pounds on her deck in plain sight. The Robalo could carry up to eight thousand pounds, but they only loaded six to keep the load lighter, and they could get into shore faster and then return to help some of the others lighten their loads so they could all finish the job quicker. They arrived back around the Loss Man River area when they lost steering on the Robalo, so Joe and Kent flagged Bobby to come over to them, and they took the other boat and put Bobby, the captain on the robalo, and a couple of crewmen on the boat.

The boat was loaded with six thousand pounds of marijuana on board when Kent told Bobby to take the boat ashore. Joe and Kent took off in the final boat and finished offloading while everyone else had gone on and left them behind.

In the meantime, when Kent left Bobby, he told him he would be right back and bring another boat and get the stuff off the boat and pick them guys up. Bobby then heard a boat in the distance, and Bobby knew that the other boats didn't know where his boat was located. He knew he had to do something quickly, so he slipped off the boat and got in the water and kept the lighter dry and would flick it off and on periodically to show them where the boat was located. He did this until the other boat came over and picked him up where they offloaded the marijuana in the other boat, and then Bobby asked the other boat's captain what happened to Kent. He should have already been back.

Joe and Kent cut straight across Mossman's, running the boat in the direction of Pavilion. They were a mile and a half offshore when a northwestern started to come down on them; the wind was blowing like crazy, and the rain had started, with seas at four feet high, and the engine stalled with water in the gas. Now, this was where the bow of the boat took a nosedive into a wave, and Kent ran to the back of the boat and started throwing the ten bales overboard. The bow went down, and the stern came up and right over, and yes, she flipped. This threw Joe and Kent straight into the nasty cold water and the elements from the storm. Joe and Kent grabbed a bale and held on to it for dear life to stay afloat. The water was rough, and at times, they had no idea where they were.

Kent and Joe started swimming to a small island that they now knew as Plover. After being in the water for a long while, the boys were freezing, and Kent didn't think he could swim any further. Kent told Joe, "I am done, and I can't go on anymore or swim any further." It was one of those nights where you couldn't see two feet in front of you, and it was dark cold and raining, and you had no idea what was in the water around you. The night was one of the coldest nights in the history of the Everglades.

Joe kept encouraging him to continue to go on. He would tell him about family and friends that would be looking for them, and they would be sending help as soon as they could. Joe then looked at Kent and said, "Come on, we can go further."

Kent then released the bale and said, "I couldn't swim anymore, Joe." Kent realized just by the grace of God, they were in water up to their necks, and they could walk to shore. Kent looked at Joe and said, "Look, I couldn't even kill myself right." Kent and Joe finally made it up to the beach, and now they were cold and wet. Everything they had was wet: the lighter, cigarettes, everything. They couldn't even build a fire.

Joe looked at Kent and said, "We are going to freeze to death." Kent replied, "No, we are not."

All they had to do was find them a couple of clamshells. In the safety of the trees, they dug two holes about two and a half feet deep, six feet long, and about three feet wide. They broke some limbs with leaves on them and lined the bottom and the sides of the holes that they had dug with the clamshells. Then they put more leaves on top of them and then pulled the sand on top of that to stay warm.

The next morning when the sun came up, they got up. They were stiff and beat up, but they slowly started moving around. Boats were moving inshore, but not offshore, so there was no chance of being seen. The weather was still too rough, so that afternoon, an hour or so before it got dark, the guys waded in that frigid-cold water across to little Pavilion, which was a couple of hundred yards out from where they were, and the water only came up to their knees. The northwest wind blew the water out, so it was very low tide. Little Plover has no beach on it. Kent found a tree that had a fork, and it was connected to a heavy limb. It looked strong enough to hold him. He picked up some driftwood and leaves and made his bunk on it for the night. Joe found himself a heavy thick tree that had two limbs he could lay up against and sleep. That night about two o'clock in the morning when the tide was high, Kent's weight shifted, and limb on his tree broke, and he ended up in the water soaking wet again and very lucky he didn't break a leg or arm. Thank God, he was on the leeward side of the island, or they might have frozen to death that night.

The next day when the sun came up, Kent and Joe started moving around and started hunting for something to eat. On the second night and the second day, Joe looked at Kent and asked, "I wonder what day it is."

Kent replied, "December the 28."

"The 28," Joe said.

Kent came back and said, "Yes, today is my birthday."

That evening they moved to Buzzard Key, which was another one hundred feet closer to the channel, which gave them a better chance at being found. Unknown to Joe and Kent, the coast guard had been searching for them ever since the morning of the sinking. The coast guard, park rangers, and even helicopters up in the air were searching unbeknown to them or the family. They found the boat capsized off Plover Key. Darryl was there in another boat when the coast guard was going to right the boat and see if there were any bodies or bales of marijuana trapped in the underside of the boat.

The coast guard asked, "Whose boat is this?"

Darryl replied, "I wouldn't know until you turn it over. Because all the boats look the same."

When the boat got turned over, there was no marijuana or bodies to be seen. Everyone sighed with relief.

The coast guard looked at the family and said, "I am sorry this search is over. There is no way a human could have survived being in the water with this cold." The coast guard told the family, "I am so sorry for your loss."

This weather was the coldest night that was ever known in history to the area, and people from there were not too sure how to handle it on dry land, but in the water was a whole new game.

After a day had passed, Darrel boarded his plane and took off in search of Kent's and Joe's bodies. Darrel had felt if they could figure out what had happened and which way the currents were running, they could come up with them dead or alive. This would bring closure to the families, and if they couldn't find them alive, he wanted their bodies for an appropriate funeral service.

Another night of Kent and Joe cold and wet in the swamp. The next morning the sun was up, and Kent was walking on the oyster bars looking for something to eat, and when Kent yelled for Joe to come quick and look, there was an airplane. Kent told Joe, "I want you to confirm you see what I am." The plane was still at a distance, and then the plane went right over the top of them. When they looked up, they saw what looked like Darryl's plane. And he was flying right at them.

Darryl had one of his brothers-in-law with him, Paul. Paul was blind as a bat, and he wore these Coke bottle glasses. Paul looked at Darryl and said, "The damn wind is blowing hard, look at that tree down there swaying in the wind."

Darrel then tilted his wing and looked and said, "That it is not a tree blowing in the wind, that is Kent." Darryl was relieved to see Kent standing there, waving his jacket so they could see him. Darryl circled the area and came back over them, and he would tilt his wings back and forth, letting them know that he saw them.

All of a sudden, another fisherman named Sheldon saw what Darryl was doing. He came over in his boat to see what was going on. Sheldon looked and could see Kent and Joe standing on the small island. Sheldon then realized that these were the boys that had been missing from a boating accident from days before. The closer he got, the happier he got because he could see the guys were beaten up from the weather, cold, and hungry, but both were in pretty good shape, giving what they had encountered the last several days. In the meantime, Darryl flew home and got his boat and headed out there as quick as he could. Sheldon then proceeded to pick up Joe and Kent off the end of the rock on the island. Darryl met up with Sheldon about halfway into the route home and took Kent and Joe off the boat to head into the family.

Before they left, Sheldon asked if there was anything on the island, and Kent said, "Yes, there is one bale in the trees. You could have it, and then you can figure out the tides and then you should be able to figure out where the bales floated off to." And he told him he could have all of it for his pay for helping them out.

Sheldon said, "I have cigarettes and soda pop, please help yourself."

Kent then told the man he would be forever grateful. They got on Darryl's boat and left heading to the house.

The moral to the story is that if Kent and Joe had kept swimming, they would have made it home just in time to attend their funeral because the townspeople had given them up for dead, and they were already planning a memorial service in their honor.

CHAPTER TEN

Mullet Fishing

One day of the captains wanted to go mullet fishing, and they took a boat into the area where they had hidden the marijuana after the last job. Upon entry into the creek, they were spotted and watched, and when they exited the area, they again were watched. The man who saw them went to the ranger station and reported them looking suspicious, and the park rangers moved in and busted the whole job, all because this captain wanted to go mullet fishing. The people who were watching the load to make sure it was safe and no one had stolen the load scrambled and took off swimming back to Chokoloskee Island as soon as they heard the boats and the helicopters coming into the area.

Everything was hot, and the law was everywhere. The Andersons got their load busted off Goodland. Another big boat had to throw another twenty thousand pounds off Pavilion. We were sitting around talking about it, and they asked what we are going to do. Darryl and Craig got in the airplane, and they flew up and out in the gulf and contacted *The Sally Ann*.

"Change of plans I have found pompano, and I am going to drop you a reading in a water bottle."

They said to pick it up. They asked, "Do you understand? This is Jewel Key." And they said yes.

They came on and said, "Have everything on the deck, we have a lot of sharks around." And it continued to say, "Don't play around, we need to have everything ready to go."

When they left the dock, and they we're told not to follow the other boats, everyone went in different directions. They all met up at Jewel Key at around ten o'clock in the evening. They sat and waited on the boat, and then the radio call came in: "Flaco, Flaco, are you there, come on." The boat got there, and it was known throughout the whole crew not to play around. They had very little time, and they know they were going to put it up a creek and which one it was. They offloaded the big boat and loaded all the small ones within an hour.

They all got together, and they knew not to make any noise. The creek was not even a mile away from Chokoloskee. Whenever it cooled off where they could move it because it was right there, and they could get to it very easy and hide it. Everyone got to the creek, and they used brown and green tarps to cover everything up to camouflage it, so it was undetectable, and they would always leave two men to watch over everything and keep it safe so the stuff would not get stolen, or if it did, they would let them know who took it.

Two days went by, and the law was still around, and another one of the captains decided he wanted to go mullet fishing. The captain went out to the creek in a smaller boat. He moved everything from one boat to another so he could take his boat out. Unknown to him, the captain was seen on his way out of the creek. Then the law enforcement came in and found where the marijuana had been hidden, and they started the boats and took them straight to the park rangers' station.

Now the family was down to one boat, and now they had to take the time to get a new one. There was a guy in Naples building a better boat called a Thornton. It was faster, sleeker, and better built and would make it run faster with the same motor.

The family had contacted Mr. Thornton, and he had already built four boats, and they placed an order for three more. It took him about three weeks to build the others to their specifications.

In the meantime, they had a job coming in from a freighter off-shore, but they had no smaller boats to offload the bigger crab boat, and if they missed this freighter, the Colombians would be very upset with the crew. Not knowing what to do, they sat down and started talking to a captain who ran offshore, by the name of Malcolm. He asked where they were going to bring the job ashore. At that time, Malcolm was told that they had no smaller boats ready, so this had to be a long haul and straight to the dock. Malcolm was a captain who was fearless and scared of nothing, and he knew the water better than anyone in the area.

He went to pick the job up, and two nights later, Malcolm brought the boat ashore right up Chokoloskee Pass next to a deep-water seawall on the island, and everyone pulled up in their vans and offloaded him right there. As soon as the boat was emptied, he took a crew hand back offshore and cleaned the boat and returned it to the spot at the dock where it once was tied. On this particular job, Malcolm was tipped an extra one hundred thousand dollars for bailing the Daniels crew out of a jam. The closing comments were this was a damned expensive mullet fishing trip. Glad it was over.

CHAPTER ELEVEN

The Saltwater Cowboys

Craig went to jail on a weapons charge after purchasing a gun from a friend that was illegal. He was sentenced to eighteen months of state time. During the time he was incarcerated, Kent continued to work the jobs and split the money with his brother. After every job, Kent would take half of the money he earned and deliver it to his wife, Gwen, at their home. No matter what the clan was, they always took care of each other in a time of need, and they were never greedy.

Randal now had the task of taking over the head position of the family and now relied on Darrel for his assistance from time to time. Randal knew the backcountry better than any of the others in the family. That was why Randal's specialty was in dire need and was brought in to figure out all the routes to take that nobody else knew.

At Pavilion, everybody was sitting there waiting for the *Popeye* to come in. The boat was a sixty-five-foot shrimp boat with no tower, outriggers, or rigging on it. It moved through the water calm and steady.

In the cover of the night, it was dark and wet, raining like crazy. All the crew huddled up in the smaller boats trying to keep warm until *The Popeye* arrived. Finally, they were contacted from the mother boat, and all of the smaller boats moved at once to get there and start offloading her. After half of the boats were offloaded on the smaller boats, Kent jumped off his boat and onto the *Popeye* and walked forward to the cabin. Checking the radar, Kent noticed there were five blotches around the boat moving toward them. Kent took that to be the coast guard and other lawmen surrounding the vessel to attempt a bust. Kent ran back outside and told his dad to get up there now and look at the radar. Kent told his dad they needed to get this shit off this boat and get the hell out of there. They got everything offloaded, and they took the three crewmen off the *Popeye*, and they left the vessel deserted with no one aboard. Kent had two crewmen with him. At this point, it was every boat for themselves. They knew where to go and what they needed to do with the cargo. Kent had a Colombian on board to watch the job to make sure the job came through or was busted so that he could report back to his people.

They would be placed there to make sure the Colombian side was protected and report back as to the progress of the job to the people he worked. If the job were busted and made the local papers, they would send the articles back to their bosses and clear the Daniels clan of their debt, but if it wasn't, you had better move the marijuana because they would be looking for their money.

Everybody got in their boats and ran in all different directions. The blue lights were all around the boats flashing. The only thing Kent could do was run from the Pavilion area to Lumbar Key and try to get into the shallow water and into the mangroves. Kent came across a boat that shined a spotlight on the water. Kent grabbed his light and blinded the man by shining his light back in his face to hold him. He held two fingers up on his right hand. Kent told his crew to throw three. He figured a small price to pay to getaway. He was the head park ranger, and he retrieved the bales from the water and allowed Kent and his crew to pass right on by. Kent went through Lumbar Key Cove heading to Rabbit Key Pass.

Just before Kent got to Rabbit Key Pass, he saw a helicopter coming their way with a spotlight shining bright. It is still dark, raining, and cold, so the visibility was very poor. Kent took the boat and slid under the trees as quick as he could to camouflage the boat from the helicopter and keep it out of view. Just as he did, it flew right over the top of them, shinning their lights almost directly on them, but it never slowed down and never saw them. Kent then took the boat out of the trees, and they hauled ass again from Rabbit Key Pass to Fish Hawk Pass because they had a lot of oyster bars and sand bars and mud, very shallow water. Kent felt as though it was a great place to hide and no one could chase him because of the knowledge of the shallow waterways.

Just about a mile away from Fish Hawk Pass, two boats came out Rabbit Key Pass coming from Everglades City. The way the boats were running and the way they were cutting through the water, Kent knew it was marine patrol and park rangers. As fast as Kent could get this motor to go, he opened it up, and they threw the blue lights on them. They were easily tracked that night because of the trail of foam they left in the water. Kent always carried a gill net on the back end of his boat for times just like this. Kent could have the crew throw the net and let it go in hopes the boats chasing them would get tangled up in them. Now the well boat, when it hit shallow water, it gained about seven miles an hour in speed, and Kent was starting to hit more shallow water than before. Fish Hawk Pass was hard to get into because you had a sharp left and a sharp right when the crew yelled, "Do you want me to throw the net?"

"No, leave it for the last resort. I have something else in mind."

Making the first left-hand turn then the right, the first boat behind Kent was a marine patrol. He made the sharp left, but he didn't make the sharp right, which put him aground close to the mangroves and on top of an oyster bar. That left the park ranger behind them, and he was coming on strong.

Fish Hawk Pass is a treacherous area. Local people know they would need to stay to the right in the deeper water. But there was a shallow pass with just enough water in it for their boat to pass between the two oyster bars, and the locals were the only ones who knew how to maneuver through it. Knowing the park ranger was going to follow Kent and not take the right-hand side. He played right into his trap. He ran aground, and Kent got to deep water and slowed the boat down and turned around, and the crew look at Kent and asked, "What the HELL are you doing?"

He went back about fifty yards where they had run aground. He picked up the spotlight, shined it on them so it would blind them, and they could not see who was in the boat when Kent asked, "Are you boys okay?."

The park ranger replied, "We are fine, just fucking fine."

"Thanks."

Kent then left and got the boat back on top and ran to Chokoloskee and to Odolph's house, where he had a Ted shed right on the sea wall with deep water access. All the marijuana was placed inside the shed, and he told Cecil to take the boat offshore and clean it out and take the boat to the dock and tie it up, and Kent told him to go home and call it a night. Kent was sitting there waiting for the other boats. Down the road he could see car lights coming towards the house, and Kent felt this couldn't be a good thing. The Colombian man picked up a light and shined it towards the area where they saw the car lights. He didn't understand. Knowing in Kent's mind, it was the law. They were on the water, why wouldn't they be on the land.

Kent took and hit the foreigner in the head and knocked him out, and he took the light and turned it off. Kent then shut the door to the shed and hid inside. They could see the light turn in towards the shed. Kent's suspicions were right; it was the law. After several minutes, the cops left. After a couple more minutes, Kent told Oddie, "We have to get out of here."

Kent knew he had his truck parked at his dad's house. They started walking through the woods, making sure no one could see them. Once they got to the truck, they took the Columbian into Everglades City. The Circle K was open twenty fours house a day. Kent asked Oddie to go inside to get something to eat and drink and cigarettes whatever he thought they might need. They drove back to Chokoloskee. There at Kent's mom and dad's house, they sat at the table. Soon Dad came in. Kent looked at his dad and asked, "You made it."

"Yes, we made it, but it was rough. Law was everywhere."

Kent asked his dad, "Where you put your load?"

Randal replied, "We hid it in the trees." Randal asked, "What did you do with yours?"

Kent replied, "I put it in Odolph's shed."

Randal replied, "We have to get it the hell out of there. The law will find it."

Kent replied, "Let's get a van and get her loaded."

Randal responded, "We couldn't do it tonight. We will have to do it first thing in the morning."

The van was brought over. It was a fifteen-passenger van with no windows, one ton with airbags so the van would stay sitting level. Got it loaded, and they told the driver to take it out.

The driver responded, "I am not going to take it. This town is too hot."

Kent asked the driver if he would drive a van loaded with the block, which was a decoy that gave Kent the time he needed to drive the other truck out of town and keep the heat off him. The driver agreed.

Kent then took the van loaded with the marijuana into Homestead and turned around and brought it back empty and learned the cops did stop the decoy van and searched it and held it for a couple of hours on the side of the road.

This was how the news media outlet tagged the Daniels family with the name "The Saltwater Cowboys." The townspeople were so pleased that the family outran all of law enforcement. They gave them a party to celebrate the victory of the job. In the newspaper the following days, a reporter nicknamed the clan after eluding the police and the law for as long as they did that night. "The Saltwater Cowboys" or the "Ghost People of Everglades" was the name that would be stuck to them for the rest of their lives.

CHAPTER TWELVE

Job Busted

It was a new day and a new job. This job was brought up through Indian Key Pass and was just short of Jenkins Key. They offloaded the job. All total, there were forty thousand pounds, which meant five thousand on each boat. Some of the boats were to go to the Barron River to Everglades Fish House. When the boats would get loaded, everybody would wait on each other when crossing the bay. Everybody in a single file, and Ivan started heading up the Barron River in Everglades City. Now some of the stuff went up the Barron River, and the rest of the boats hid it in the mangroves because they could not bring it in all at one time. They got almost into the Rod and Gun Club, and a cop had driven down River Road. When he turned the corner heading south, his eyes were big when he saw six boats loaded with marijuana coming up the Barron River. He never turned the blue light on, but they knew it was not one of the deputies that they had bought off. When the deputy eased off and left, and the crew was already asking what they were going to do, they knew they were busted.

Kent could see some of the other crew jumping off the boats ahead of him swimming in. "Let's get them and get to the offloading area at the fish house."

They offloaded the stuff into two semi-trucks that were sitting there waiting at the dock. They cleaned the boat because they knew they were busted, and they didn't want to take a chance and leave anything on board. There was only one narrow passage to get away. Kent looked at his dad and said, "I would see you in the morning. I am going to head out on Anika and hit the river and go to Turners River and run it all the way home."

Randal asked Kent if he thought there was enough water to run the boat. And he said yes. It was airboat trails, and they were cut in with no grass. He asked his dad what he was going to do. "I guess I'm going to turn her around and head to Chokoloskee Bay, and there is nothing on this boat." A lot of people just left their boats sitting there.

The captains did not want to take a chance. By the time Kent got his boat back to Chokoloskee, he had cleaned it up, but by the time sunrise came, the boat was tied to the dock. The next morning, the law moved in on the drugs, but all the people had left; no drivers or captains were anywhere around. They all were gone. It always helps when you had the law in your back pocket. They waited three nights before returning to retrieve the stuff that was put in the woods. And they took it into Lanes River and took it across Panther Creek and loaded it on johnboats to some semi-truck that was set up to move the stuff. Just north of corners town, and then it was sent out to Homestead to be moved out and sold so the crew could be paid what they were owed for the job.

*****

The following night, Kent and a friend of his named Pete decided to go pompano fishing. Pete had seen a large school earlier that day. Pete and Kent had talked, and he had felt like there would be about five thousand pounds, if not more, of fish in that strike. Pete had explained to Kent where he had seen the fish, and he thought it would be an easy catch. You see, pompano had a compressed body with a short snout that was silver with yellow on its side and the fins and tail. When the fish jumped, they referred to this as the fish was skipping in the water. Kent then talked to Pete and concluded that they needed to get another hand on the boat to help pull the net. He told Kent, "Let's to get Joey Boy." Kent's adopted nephew.

They left the dock at nine o'clock that evening. It was a clear calm night; the weather that they had experienced the night before had finally passed. Heading out on the boat to Sand Fly Pass and then to Jewel Key, getting out in the area where Pete had seen the pompano. Turning the skip light on and shinning it in the water off the back of the boat.

When you looked for pompano skipping across the water, it looked like a kid throwing a flat rock across the water, and it skipped like a stone. The motor of a boat could startle them and make them start moving and skipping, driving them towards deep water with the net sitting just off the bank.

Whenever Pete flipped the light on, the fish started skipping, and then all hell broke loose with other boats in the area that they could not see. Pete yelled, threw the Bowie to the net, which had a light on it to let you know where the end of the net was. They could hear in the distance boats starting up and diesel engines coming on and the outboard motors on the boats starting to fire up. Boats were everywhere and all around them, but they could not see them. The boats were running in all directions, but they still could not see them. The boat sounds were coming from all around them now, but the engine noise was everywhere, and this all happened at the time the pompano started skipping across the water. They knew it was going to be a good and bountiful strike, but the boats were still going in all different directions. Again, they could hear them, but they couldn't see them; it was very dark and a black night. You could not see beyond the edge of the boat. They then started running net off the back of the boat to lay off the side of the bank to catch the pompano. Now they had about two hundred yards of the net overboard, and when the boat was about halfway through what was on board, the boat started hitting things in the water. Pete slowed the boat down and grabbed the spotlight, and he yelled at Kent to cut the net.

Kent looked at him and said, "What is wrong?"

Pete then said, "Get up here. And look for yourself."

When Kent got to the area where he could shine his light in the water, they could see all of these bales floating. Apparently, with the light and the noise from the boats that they heard, they had interrupted a crew offloading a marijuana job being done by an outside organization. The outside crew got spooked and threw the job, and now these bales were everywhere. The guys were unaware of any job going on, so the guys were surprised.

They were making this job fair game for anyone to pick up. The guys decided that with Pete running the boat, Kent and Joey Boy started picking up the bales and started stacking them on the boat. After they got about twelve thousand pounds, they took the boat straight and hid the stuff in the woods out of sight in the mangroves.

The next morning, Pete and Joey Boy went back out to get the net, and the pompano had cut it the night before. While Kent went and told Randal and explained to him what had happened, Randal got up and made coffee while Kent was drinking tea. Kent told his dad that there was a job that got thrown, and he asked Kent how did he know. Kent explained to his dad that they had gone pompano fishing, and they had scared a crew that wasn't from this area.

Randal asked, "You didn't do it on purpose, did you?"

Kent said, "No, I wouldn't do that, but we got about twelve thousand pounds in the woods, and if you want to get any more of it, then we need some more boats, and we need to get going."

Randal asked, "How many boats you think we are going to need?"

And Kent replied, "Yours, mine, and one more."

They went and got the boats ready, and Randal called Bobby and said, "Get up and get ready. We have something we need to take care of." He asked him to bring the crew. After confirmation that they were ready to go, they took off from the docks and headed out to the area. They got there and used dim lights and started picking up the bales and stacking it on the boats. As the boats were filled, they took the bales to the upper creek and stacked it in the woods so it could be moved and shipped out.

*****

After they finished retrieving the bales from the thrown job, Randal told the crew that they had to fuel the boats back up and have them ready. They left that evening heading to the little pavilion, and it was still a dark, clear night, and the wind was out of the south. A million stars were shining in the sky on this clear night, and they were shining bright. There were five boats the crew was running, and now they had gathered up at Little Pavilion waiting for the boat coming towards them to offload the twenty thousand pounds that she was hauling to meet them. While Kent was sitting there, he was gazing at the sky and looking at the Big Dipper and the Little Dipper, and he was remembering his forefathers teaching him how to navigate by the stars, and the North Star in particular, when he noticed a bright shooting star running across the sky, and then he thought to himself how amazing it was to have such a beautiful clear night and how lucky he was to have grown up in such a majestic place.

They sat there until one o'clock in the morning, and the boat was a no-show, so now at three o'clock in the morning, the crew decided to head back to the dock. Then the next morning, Kent went back over to his dad and was asking what had happened to the boat.

Randal replied, "We have the airplane up in the air trying to contact the boat." A couple of hours later, Randal got the news that the boat was broken down.

He looked at Kent and told him that they had to get that stuff off the boat and get it in. Kent responded, "Get me to Marathon and let me pick up the *Bluebird*." Kent called Johnny and told him to get the *Bluebird* ready and to have supplies for two nights because he was flying in and would be there in a couple of hours.

Upon arrival in Marathon, Johnny picked up Kent, and they left the dock at two o'clock in the afternoon. They were heading out to the other boat, which was about a six-hour ride one way. Kent called the other boat on the radio and told them to have the tow ropes ready for them to be towed in to be fixed.

When Kent arrived, they hooked the boat up and towed it all night and the rest of the next day, and once he got them into forty feet of water, he throw his anchor because they were getting ready to transfer the load on to the bluebird.

Once they got it transferred, Kent told him that there would be a boat coming to the to help them in the morning. Kent got the job in at nine-thirty at Little Pavillion and made contact to have the other boats meet him for offloading on to the smaller boats.

Kent's crew ran his boat out to him, and Kent told Johnny to take the *Bluebird* and wash her out and take her back to Marathon put her back to dry dock. Once Kent was on board his boat he was at home at the helm and getting the load and his crew safe and to shore. They ran right up to Chokoloskee and loaded it to the box trucks and vans and sent it out to the famous meeting spot in Homestead to be shipped and sold.

CHAPTER THIRTEEN

Monkeying Around

This next job took them to Morman Key. It was a cold clear night, and the wind was light. Captain Ronnie on a shrimp boat was heading in with the cargo of choice that carried a premium price. This boat had been to Colombia and back. When it was there, it picked up eighteen thousand pounds.

Everybody met up in the designated location and were idling in anticipation of the radio call. Kent was running an hour behind them because of mechanical issues with his boat.

Kent got there at the same time the boat arrived, and Darrel and a couple of the labors were on the deck of the boat. Kent being impatient and the smartass he was, he stepped up on the deck of the boat, looked at Darrel, and said, "We are burning darkness. Let's get this stuff unloaded and get out of here." Kent then looked at Danny, one of the crewmen, and said, "Give me a hand, and let's open the ice hole hatch." Which he did. Kent told Danny to get down there, and he said, "Let's start throwing this shit out on the deck. I will help you."

Danny had one of these big wool lambskin jackets, one with a heavy collar. Kent had flicked his cigarette overboard, and it was so dark, and you really could not see in the hole where the bales were stacked. Kent climbed down the ladder into a hole that was about eight feet deep and fifteen feet wide and eighteen feet long. There were no lights in the hole; it was complete darkness. Feeling his way around, Kent found a bale and threw it up on the deck. Reached down to grab another, and Kent felt Danny shove him. Not thinking much about it because it was dark, and Kent just thought it was a mistake, so he then reached down and threw another bale on deck. Then Kent bent over to get another one, and he felt Danny kick him in the ass.

Kent replied, "You better leave me the hell alone."

Then Danny started to pinch Kent on his back. Kent was losing patience with him real quick and said, "I am going to knock the hell out of you if you don't leave me alone."

Kent reached over and grabbed Danny's big wool jacket, and he drew back and told Darrel to turn the light on. To Kent's surprise, Danny was not in the hole with him. An orangutan was standing on a couple of bales of pot. When Darrel turned the light on, Kent swung and hit the orangutan square in the jaw. The orangutan turned and looked at him and smiled. He backhanded Kent and knocked him about ten feet back. Everybody was out on the deck, including Danny, was waiting for the owner of the orangutan and getting him out of the hole, and Kent happen to go into the hole before this could happen. Now Kent was in big trouble.

Kent yelled, "What the fuck is this shit."

Darrel yelled back and said, "It's a goddamn monkey."

The orangutan would put his knuckles on the floor and swing his feet forward and knock the hell out of Kent and knock him to the floor of the boat with little to no effort at all. Kent could not get away from him. The more he tried, the more the orangutan came after him. Kent was screaming and yelling "Get him off of me. He is killing me."

Kent would get to the ladder and try to climb out of the hole, and the monkey would let him get to the top and pull him back down again. It was like a game the orangutan was playing with Kent.

He would kick him, bite him, and pounce on top of him. After a while, when Kent thought he could not handle any more, this man came running to the back of the boat and turned the lights on where the monkey was and started yelling, "Did the bad man hurt my baby. Come to Daddy." And the orangutan came running out of the hole and jumped in the man's arms and started weeping. The man kept asking, "Did the bad man hurt you?" And the orangutan wept like a baby.

The deckhands helped Kent get out of the hole, and Darrel asked, "How did that work out for you. Did you get him? It was just a little monkey."

Kent said, "The little monkey whipped my ass."

After an hour and a half, Oddie had to run the boat because Kent's face was so badly beaten he couldn't see. His eyes were completely swollen shut, and when he got home, his mother did not recognize him.

To this day, Kent would not go into the hole of the boat first until he made sure he was the only one in there, and there were no monkeys around.

CHAPTER FOURTEEN

Black Jamaican Moon

Kent was home one evening sleeping, and Randal came in one night and awoke him.

Randal said, "Son, and we have a problem."

Kent replied, "What's wrong?"

"We took the money from one job and financed another." Randal said, "The job is on the beach, and the law is around it."

"Okay, what do you need out of me?" Kent replied.

"I have a boat and captain, but nobody that will go down because they are all scared."

"Okay, who's the captain?"

He said, "Malcolm."

Kent told him to tell Malcolm to meet him at the airport in the morning. "Tell him I will go down with him to pick it up."

In the morning, they arrived at the airport and took off to Marathon Key. After arriving, they had to make sure the boat was fueled and iced up and had enough food and drinks for seven days.

"Don't forget the alcohol and cigarettes," Malcolm replied.

"I got you covered," Kent said.

Just after dark, they eased away from the dock and headed out to Port Antonio, Jamaica.

Once they left the United States waters, they lost all the Laurence C readings. Unlike the new GPS systems, they worked off radio towers, and once they entered international waters, all navigation was done by charts and compass to plot their course.

The next day on the other side of Cuba, next to the Cayman Islands, the boat came across a pod of whales. These whales were known as the False Killer Whale. They lived in the warm tropical waters that they all seemed to enjoy.

Malcolm and Kent cut the engine and let the boat drift, and they sat and watched the whales jump across the bow of the boat and bump the bottom of the boat, and they would shove the boat around and then go under it and lift it up and then dropped it back into the water. They splashed and played for approximately forty-five minutes, and just as they appeared, they disappeared as quick as they came. Kent and Malcolm enjoyed watching this during the trip. It was something that neither of them had ever encountered before.

That night, approximately five miles from Jamaica, the engine started to overheat. They had to start to check the engine to try to figure out why the engine was hot. The first thing they needed to check to see was if the screen on the bottom of the intake for the saltwater used to cool the engine was clogged, so at around one the next morning, Kent decided he needed to go overboard, and he took a brush to make sure it was clear of any debris. The water depth was approximately eleven hundred feet deep. With deep water came the fear of being eaten by something unknown. After checking the intake valve, they realized it was not the problem. They now realized it was the freshwater pump that had gone out.

They had to make their way into port with this broken boat slowly. They came ashore in Ocho Rios, Jamaica. They pulled into a dock and fueled up the tanks. Their security met them at the dock, and they had to explain they were commercial fishermen, fishing outside the Cayman Islands, and their boat had broken down, and they had to come to the nearest port and get parts flown to them. Security told them not to leave the boat. The next morning they were met by their customs agents, five of them and three German Shepard dogs dressed all in white with white gloves. They got on the boat and went from bow to stern, and if anyone knew about a Detroit Diesel, if she wasn't leaking oil, she wasn't running, so when they entered the engine room, their pretty white suites were no more; they were smeared and blotted in oil. They asked them some questions, and they asked how long they were going to be there.

Kent replied, "As long as it takes to get apart." Kent asked if there were any Detroit Diesel parts around.

The man replied, "No."

They then asked if they had a telephone they could use to get parts flown to them. So they used the phone and called the United States and had the part flown into them.

The next day, they got the part; Kent put the pump on.

Back on their way again heading toward Port Antonio, Jamaica. They got into the port and pulled up to the customs dock and tied off. Kent was lying in the top bunk in the wheelhouse, and he was reading a *Penthouse* magazine. Out of the corner of his eye, every so often, he would catch a glimpse of something in the window, but when he looked, there was nothing there. Kent then turned over on his side when he saw the head start coming up in the window. Kent grabbed him by the hair and asked him what he was doing. The young boys started pointing to the magazine he was holding, so Kent gave the boy the magazine. Thinking it was funny, Kent got up and had a mixed drink and lit a cigarette, still with his eye on the young boy and his book. He left the dock and would show people the pictures in the book, and he would tear them out and sell them anywhere from three to five dollars apiece. The little boy came back and showed Kent the money he made from the book.

Malcolm looked at his and said, "What are you doing."

They had a *Playboy*, and the boy wanted another book, so Kent gave him that one. The only thing he would say about this matter is if he owned a *Playboy* or *Penthouse*, he would hire this little boy because he knew how to make money with their magazines.

It was getting later in the afternoon, and Customs came and asked them what they were doing and how long they were going to be there.

"Three or four days."

They asked them their business.

They replied, "We are commercial fishermen using traps off the Cayman Islands." And they needed fuel and ice. They told them it was an election year, and they would have to go to the center of the bay and anchor up and fly a red flag. To mark the boat as not being checked in or not registered yet. They told them they had no red flags on the boat, so the Customs told them to fly anything they had that was red. After looking around the boat, the only thing that was red on the boat was a pair of red boxer shorts that belonged to Malcolm. Let's say they were big enough to be seen.

The next morning about seven in the morning, they called them back to the dock and told them they could take the red flag down and checked them in. They told them they could go over to the yacht club, but they could not leave the concrete of the club, and they were warned it was an election year and if they stepped on the grass or anything else, they could be shot. Malcolm and Kent got over to the yacht club and got tied up the first tie. They had stepped off the boat in four days onto dry land.

The yacht club had a bar and showers where the guys could clean up. They needed their clothes washed, so the bartender told them of a local lady who would wash their clothes and bring them back to them. Once they got their clothes, they could shower and feel like human beings again. That evening, the bar filled up with a few people, and they were having a good time talking with them, and they met a couple who asked them if they wanted to go fishing with them on their boat. Which they responded yes, they would love it. Another guy said that he had flown down in a twin-engine plane to pick up fifteen hundred pounds of pot and fly it back to the States. He got down there and got drunk and spent the money and didn't even have enough money to buy fuel for the plane. The next morning, the guys were up and on the boat fishing with their new Jamaican friends. This was the first time Kent had ever been sail fishing in his life, so he thought it was interesting. After being out there for a couple of hours, this plane flew very low across the bow of the boat, and then he did it again. Then they noticed it was the guy from the bar with the plane.

Kent looked at Malcolm and the other people. "I thought he didn't have enough fuel to fly the plane."

Everyone agreed. The airplane made another pass down the side of the boat. One of the engines stopped, and the other one started to spit and sputter. He ran the plane out of fuel, and he landed on the belly of the plane in the water; within a couple of minutes, the plane sunk to the bottom. Kent and Malcolm helped the pilot get to the safety of the boat.

Going back to the yacht club sitting around the bar, everyone was talking, laughing, and having a good time. On the music box they had, they were playing county music. From the outside walked eight people. They sat at the bar and visited with the new people that came in. One of the guys that just came in asked, "Do you like reggae music?"

Kent replied, "Yes, I am very fond of it."

Kent told the guy that there was one guy liked, and Kent responded, "I like Jimmy Cliff."

Everyone in the bar started laughing. They asked him, "Have you ever met Jimmy Cliff?"

Kent replied, "I have listened to his music, but I have never had the pleasure of meeting the man."

Then this man stood up and shook Kent's hand and said, "I am Jimmy Cliff."

That evening when the yacht club was closing for the night, they asked the club to sell them bottles of alcohol and the mixes so they could continue the party on the boat.

There were fifteen people on this forty-foot boat other than Malcolm and Kent. Let's say the endangered species rocked it out that night.

But before the night was over, this young woman came up and asked if there was a restroom she could use. They guys said no, they locked the restrooms at night. She asked where she was going to pee. She had to go. Malcolm said, "Just go to the back of the boat and grab the leg of the shade, pull your pants down, and squat over the side and pee."

The girl had no choice, so she did as she was told. During the process of going to the bathroom, her pants around her ankles, and no one feeling any pain and listening to music, this girl's hand slips, and she fell overboard. Which everyone thought it was funny until someone yelled, "She couldn't swim."

Malcolm said, "Oh shit."

And they went to the wheelhouse and grabbed the spotlight that was mounted to the ceiling, but it had a handle where you could adjust the light up and down where you could see. Malcolm shined the spotlight looking for the girl. It was a dark black night. After a few minutes of searching and hunting for her off to the side of where Malcolm had the light, Kent started seeing these ripples on the water, and he will tell you now that you have never seen a prettier sight than a black Jamaican moon on the rise glistening in the water. She was face down, and her pants were still down around her ankles. It was a sight to behold knowing that she was okay.

They finished the party up, and they were laughing and joking about the black Jamaican moon. The next morning around ten o'clock, some more people came by the boat, and Kent asked was there any place they could get fuel. He was they had already been taken care of, with the fuel will be here later this afternoon. That's what they came down here to let them know. The guy came down to the boat, and he confirmed the destination of where the pickup was.

Kent asked him about how hot the law was around the pickup, and the guy responded by showing him a badge and replying, "We are the law, and we are the ones you have been buying from."

Kent got tickled and said, "Well, then all right. Then let's go get it."

The guy looked at Kent and asked, "Do you what to smoke some ganja with us."

"While in Jamaica, do as the Jamaicans do."

He broke out this large brown paper and rolled it in a cone shape.

Kent got a kick out of looking at the ganja being rolled and as soon as they finished, then they fired it up, and needless to say, it kicked Malcolm and Kent's asses. Let's say they were up in smoke that early afternoon.

Later that afternoon, the fuel truck came out to the boat. They filled the tanks on the boat with two thousand gallons of fuel. They said their goodbyes, and they pulled away from the dock, and they were blasting Jimmy Cliff's "I Can See Clearly Now" as they were heading out.

After they got to where they were supposed to pick up the marijuana, this guy came out in a long canoe called a banana boat, and he had some of the pot on his boat. Kent caught a glimpse of sparkle on the man's chest. Kent grabbed the man and hit him and threw him overboard. The other man with a hood on yelled "What in the hell is wrong with you."

Kent replied, "Why, we have the law on our boat."

The man responded, "The law is who you buy the marijuana from."

After the pot was loaded and Kent looked at Malcolm, here was an appropriate song for them to listen to on their way out of there: "Many Rivers to Cross" by Jimmy Cliff.

On the way back, the guys hit Cuba just about dark. They turned and headed to the north around the Cape of Hope in Cuba. The boat slapped fifteen-foot seas in the face in the forty-eight-foot boat. They got sideways in the seas and started taking on water, so they had to get inshore of the reef next to the beach, and it was already dark. They got inshore the reefs and pumped the water out and let them dry out, and the next morning at daylight, they started looking around, and it looked like they were next to a misled base. Knowing that if they were caught in their waters off Cuba and being a vessel from the United States, it would be hell to pay, Malcolm and Kent decided they had no choice but to leave the safety of where they were. The seas were still topping out at eight to ten feet.

At this point, Kent was running the boat, and Malcolm was lying in the bunk. Back offshore, they started hitting waves, and the boat went up, and the bow went down, and just about the time he was about to ask Malcolm a question, they hit a bigger wave, and Malcolm came out of the bunk and hit the floor. Malcolm had a bad back, and Kent figured this would just about kill him with pain. About an hour later and leaving Cuban waters and entering the international waters from Cuba, Kent looked up and saw a two-hundred-foot ship with an orange stripe halfway down the side of her. Kent was looking out through a pair of binoculars and concluded that it was a cruise ship.

Malcolm looked up and saw it and yelled "Coast guard!"

Kent started hunting the coast guard that Malcolm was yelling about when Malcolm pointed to the cruise ship. Kent looked at him and said, "That is not a coast guard, it's a cruise ship. Look, don't you see all the girls in bikinis."

"Oh thank God," Malcolm replied.

Finally, the next night they were sitting at Rabbit Key being unloaded by their crew. The job came ashore with no issues.

CHAPTER FIFTEEN

A Hot Commodity

The Everglades became a hot commodity these days. The newfound fame and money took the city to a whole new level and attitude called greed. Now there were several groups of people hauling pot through the Ten Thousand Islands, joining the new industry that had made its way into this area.

Word got out that two larger crab boats were busted offshore and being brought in. One had fifteen thousand pounds on it, and the other was carrying twenty thousand pounds. During the chase, the bales got thrown overboard, and there was pot floating everywhere. The boats and the job belonged to other organizations that worked in this industry as well.

The law and the heat were everywhere. Cops were crawling the streets and the waterways looking for any movement. They had roadblocks coming in and going out of the small island. Cars were being stopped and searched. Tempers flew from the local people of the city because they were a tight niche community or clan, and they didn't like outsiders or people probing into their personal life or business.

Once the bust came into play, the law focused the majority of their time on the busted boats, so this allowed the Daniels crew to move swiftly and get their load ashore.

The area was called the Last Frontier, and the Daniels crew had the reputation of being the cowboys of the water, and no one knew the area better than they did, and they knew the area was hot before they left the dock. They could not take the chance of leaving their crew and boat offshore as a sitting duck waiting to be busted. They took two boats at a time and with extra crew onboard to offload the marijuana on to the smaller boats as quickly as they could. They continued this until the big boat was empty.

They ran the pot slow and steady, making their way through Jewel Creek, making as little noise as possible so the load could be taken into Chokoloskee Island and dropped at Billy's place and stacked until they could bring dump trucks in to haul it out of there.

They brought the trucks in one at a time, and they loaded the bales into the bottom of them and covered them with the rock that the trucks normally carried.

After they felt they had enough and the trucks didn't look too heavy or overloaded, they drove the marijuana to the roadblocks, and with the law enforcement officer waving them through, they drove straight to Homestead and collected their money for one of the most outrageous hauls ever.

The next morning, the Daniels crew got together and decided that it was fair game to go out there and pick up any of the bales that were thrown from the boat that was busted. Before the trip could proceed, some members of the group took a package full of money, twenty thousand to be exact, to the sheriff's office and said, "Here is a little something for you, and if you like it, this could be done once a week. We are sure you and your guys could use it, and this will be kept between us no one needs to know."

Kent and five other boats went out and picked up everything they could pick up, and they had all agreed to keep the boats as light as possible so they could run at top speeds. All boats had about 2,500 pounds apiece on board, and they picked it up in the middle of the day.

They agreed they would take it and meet up in the Stevens Pass in Port of the Islas Channel in Fekaunion, heading to the creek, which took you back to US 41, which was a hard way to get there. They still had a few hours before dark, so Kent headed offshore, and when he was around and West Pass Key and heading to Feckaunion Creek. Now when they were picking it up, there was a helicopter in the air looking for people doing this very thing. The Daniels crew had bought the law and had them in their back pocket. From now on, it made things just a little easier. They could do their job with no added hassle. After they went to meet up with the rest of the boats, they headed over to Gator Hole Bay. The water was so low and muddy from the time they picked up the job to the time they delivered the stuff. It took thirteen nights to finish the job. It almost didn't seem worth it, but regardless, the money was.

On the last night of the job getting to US 41, Kent's motor ran hot, and he blew the engine. It was shot. Now the crew had to pull, push, and shove the boat the rest of the way to the highway. They offloaded her and shoved her out of the way so the boat could not be seen. The next day, Kent went to the local outboard marina and bought a new engine for the boat and got a mechanic to put it on for him and called a friend of his who had a wrecker. The motor was unbolted, and the new bolted in, and within an hour, they were going again.

A pound of marijuana was worth about three hundred dollars per pound, and they had fifteen thousand pounds, so I think you can do the math and see the amount of money running through the veins of the Everglades.

CHAPTER SIXTEEN

The Laci Lady Purchase

Through the years, the one thing that the Daniels clan did was maintain other legal business interests. The *Gulf Pride*, purchased and financed through the bank, the *Gulf Pride*, was a forty-three-foot Torrez Haul boat, which was equipped with 1292 turbo Detroit Diesel engine with the legal proceeds from crabbing and the lobster (Florida crawfish) business. There was the local fish house called Everglades Seafood to help Kent purchase all of the equipment that was needed for him to get started in the business. They helped by financing the operation for him, as well.

Randal bought the *Eighty Proof*, which was a fifty-one-foot commercial fishing boat used for crabbing and the lobster business as well.

As long as Kent owned the boat called the *Gulf Pride*, he never used her to smuggle marijuana through the Everglades or do anything illegal.

This is just a blanket statement but one that needs to be said. The Daniels family were smart, savvy businessmen, whether it was the smuggling of marijuana or running a legitimate fishing business—it was running to be profitable, and profitable it was.

Throughout time to time, Kent would make the trip to Bogota, Jamaica, and Belize offshore, picking up from freighters. Kent didn't go offshore just for the fun of it. Through the time Kent spent with Malcolm, who was one of the best captains who had ever lived and came out of the Everglades area, Malcolm took Kent under his wing and taught him everything he knew he knows to date.

Now, Kent had a wit about him, and he knew how to handle all types of situations and how to navigate the water from country to country.

Kent got in the airplane and went to Marathon to look at a boat that was for sale named *The Boss Lady*. The boat wasn't to his liking, so Kent went to a local bar called Fara Blanco and had a couple of drinks with Marshall and Johnny. While sitting there, he overheard a conversation between another man and two others that were sitting a couple of bar stools down. They were talking about finding some sucker who would buy his boat with all of his fishing gear. He said if he could find someone that would buy it all, he would sell it. The man carried on this conversation going back and forth for a while. Kent then went and asked the men the location of the boat and he then pointed out the window and said there she was tied to the dock.

Kent then asked the man selling the boat why did they want to get rid of her? The man replied nothing was wrong with her. "Nothing, I just had one of the engines rebuilt at has 1292 twin-turbo diesel engines, and she runs well."

Kent looked perplexed and said then why.

The man replied, "I have been down on my luck, and I haven't caught any fish all year long, and I just want to get out of the business." He said he was tired and wanted to retire. Kent then asked what he wanted for the boat and all the gear. Seventy thousand, and there were four nets and a trailer to haul the nets on. Two mackerel nets and two kingfish nets. Kent asked him if he would give him a couple of hours.

Kent then called home and spoke with his father and asked to have the money sent over. Kent went back to the bar and told the man he would take the boat and that there would be a plane that was going to fly the money over to them and it would be there soon. Kent went to the airport and met the guys with the money. He then returned to the bar and walked up to the gentleman and asked, "Do you want to count it here at the bar or do you have a room?"

A car was waiting outside in the parking lot for them, and the money was taken to the room to be counted.

Kent then walked inside the room and dumped the money on the bed and asked, "Do you want to count it?"

Kent had several men with him to make sure the money was safe and was given to the man without any problems.

The man replied, no, he didn't want to count the money. Then Kent proceeded to make the sale legal and told the man it was a documented vessel and they would have to go to Key West to change the title. The man agreed, and the next morning all parties involved in the transaction climbed in the plane and flew to Key West.

While there in Key West, Kent ran into a friend of his who worked on boats. Kent explained to him that he had just bought a seventy-five-foot boat, and he wanted him to paint the boat a light grey so it wouldn't shadow, and it would be harder to see at night. The gentleman replied, "You don't want light grey, you want this light blue that I have for you. This color works best for what you want."

Kent and the guys flew back to Marathon to get on the boat and were going to take her down to Key West.

In route on the Gulf of Mexico side down around Logger Head Island, Kent looked out the front window of the boat and saw some fish had risen to the top of the water.

He then yelled for Johnny and asked, "Do you want to take them?"

Johnny's first question was "You can get someone else to clear the net?"

When you strike kingfish, you circle the school of fish after the net was thrown, and the net would feed off the back of the boat with the let-go bowie in the circle and then purse the cork line down and pull it together and make the fish hit it. The total fish caught weighed in excess of fifty-eight thousand pounds, which just about paid for the boat.

They loaded the net with the fish back on the boat and left for the dock. They unloaded the net at the dock with the fish still in it.

Once they were there, Kent told the guy at the dock to get pickers to clear the net.

After they did that, they proceeded to Key West and dropped the boat off at the painters they had called for a car to meet them. Then they got in the car and drove back down to Marathon. The next morning, Kent went back down to Big Pine Key to see the man at the fish house, and he handed Kent a ticket and statement showing what their catch was and explained that he could pick up a check in three days.

Kent then asked the man if he knew anybody who wanted to buy the nets.

The man replied, "I am sure I can find someone."

Kent then went back to Faro Blanco with a statement in hand and walked in the bar and saw the man who he just bought the boat from sitting inside. Kent walked over and showed him the ticket.

The man asked, "Where in the hell did you catch this at?"

Kent replied, "Just off of Logger Head Key."

The man replied, "That's just my fucking luck, I sat out there for five weeks and saw nothing."

A week later the painter called back, and he said he had salvaged a navy boat that had gone down and it had a set of hydrofoils on it that he could get installed on his boat, and it fit his boat perfect.

After spending fifty thousand for routine maintenance and installing the hydrofoils on the boat, it then had to go to another man named Billy Tyner so that he could redo all of the ice box areas of the boat and put his specialty to work for the Daniels clan. He was notorious for building hideaway compartments in the boats for discretion. The crew cabin was shortened so they could hide at least twenty thousand pounds of marijuana under the deck and beside the ice hole, so if they got boarded, it would look like a bulkhead.

Billy Tyner was a master carpenter who took great pride in his work, and he had a special talent for doing things just like this. No two jobs were ever the same. Different boats required different things. Most of the organizations used him for specialty things when it came to boats. Billy's boats were sought after by many of the organizations that worked several areas up and down the state of Florida.

Now the waiting game began. Waiting for Billy to rework the boat to the specifications that Kent and he had agreed on. The wait was a really tedious job since Kent was not the most patient person in the world. They knew it would take a few months for the full completion to take place. Kent left the boat with him at an undisclosed location and then went back to Everglades City.

CHAPTER SEVENTEEN

The Parkway Campground

The Daniels crew had another job on its way. That night they had decided to try a little something different with this job coming in. Kent had to get the boats ready. And get the crew alerted to what was about to go down. The crew decided to bring the job into Parkway Campground. Randal had made an arrangement with the owner of the campground not to let anyone other than their crew camp at the point that night until they left the next day.

The Parkway Campground was an area with endless mangrove islands, which was perfect for the crew to move through the waterways undetected. The Daniels crew had three motor homes coming into the area that night, and as the boats would come ashore, they were going to be loaded. Then they were going to be taken out the next morning. No one was to be on the point except for the crew itself.

Picking up twenty thousand pounds at Little Pavilion and bringing to Chokoloskee to the point, everybody got there and started unloading into the first motor home after loading; the doors were shut and locked. The second one was loaded, and the doors were shut and locked. The prize was always behind door number three: no lights on. They opened the door and threw ten bales in the motor home when someone turned the light on, and all of a sudden, the people went to yelling, "Don't shoot, don't kill us."

One of the guys obediently went over and got Randal. Randal quickly came to the motor home and talked to the people and calmed them down. He asked, "How did you end up over here?"

The couple said the man in the office told them where to park. Randal then explained to them that they were put in the middle of something they should not have seen. Randal also told them that they could not have their keys or leave until morning. He reiterated to them that they were not going to be hurt, and they would be well compensated for their time. In the morning, Randal showed up with their keys and a duffel bag that had fifteen thousand dollars in it, and it was given to the couple for their inconvenience and trouble that they had caused them and asked for their silence.

Once the morning came and the couple was fed and then given their money that was promised, the couple seemed to calm down, and to this day, they still visit and laugh about the experience. Kent and the crew sat down with them, and after long conversations with them, they learned they were really good people and appreciated the extra money.

After a year later, they looked them up and asked if they needed to use their motor home; they could anytime. When they came back down, they would host backyard BBQ and fish fries, and they were always welcome to come on by and enjoy the family festivities. Every year from then on, they would check back with them once a year until the indictments came down in Operation Everglades One.

CHAPTER EIGHTEEN

Hostage

Today word went out that a job was thrown overboard when the law was chasing one of the other organization's boats doing a job. The Daniels crew had a meeting and decided once again they would go out in the T-craft boats and pick up as much stuff as possible that was floating.

There were twenty thousand pounds of pot floating in the water down by Rabbit Key and Pavilion by the bank. Out of the twenty thousand pounds, sixteen thousand was picked up by the Daniels crew.

The guys took all the marijuana and hid it in different locations in the woods and mangroves for safekeeping. The mangroves were so intertwined that it was virtually impossible to see the bales of marijuana or know where it was hidden unless you put it there.

It was a known rule of engagement that if a job was thrown, it was fair game for anyone to pick it up because it was thrown from the original boat that was hauling it in. If the law picked it up, it would have been confiscated.

A knock came upon the door from a Colombian man named Oscar, and he was holding a gun, and it was placed in the face of Dwain, who was part of the Daniels crew, and he was told that he would not leave or let any of the family leave unless it was in a body bag. This upset Dwain because he was not the only person in the house. The home belonged to his mom and dad, and his aunt and uncle were there visiting. Oscar then told Dwain to contact whoever he needed to because they wanted their stuff back, and they were not going to leave until they got it.

Dwain did as he was told. He called the Family and let them know they were being held hostage and at gunpoint.

The Family became very angry. Please remember this was a clan, and in time of need, they would clan up as tight as you have never seen, and God forbid if you ended up on their wrong side of that.

Within an hour, the phone rang, and Oscar, the guy representing the Colombian organization, was asked to get on the phone. Randal proceeded to tell them that he wasn't getting the stuff back unless he bought it from them outright and to please look outside. As he could see, the house was surrounded, and all guns were drawn. It was his choice now because at this point, the way they see it, he was not going to come out of that house alive. When Oscar looked, he could see about twenty to thirty people around the house; all the clan was packing, and all the guns were aimed directly at the house.

Oscar then decided to take another approach. He put his gun on the table and walked outside with his hands in the air asking for them not to shoot. Oscar left and said he needed to talk to his people, and they were going to meet just down the road they came in on, and it was going to take place on the side of that same road. A group of people from Miami came back to the area. The Daniels crew and all the people from Miami were talking on the side of the road calmly. They asked for their stuff back, and the Daniels crew informed them that this was a thrown job, and the only way they could get it back was to pay them for the job for bringing it in. After a short discussion, the Miami group decided they were going to be tough and teach these backwoods country boys a lesson and take it from them. Well, let's just say they made the biggest mistake they could have ever made. *They pulled a gun!*

One of the guns was shoved in Randal's stomach. Before the man could pull the trigger, Randal put the skin of his left hand between his thumb and forefinger right between the trigger and the firing pin to stop the gun from going off. Dwain happened to see what was going on, and he came running over and hit the man on the side of his face and hitting him on the temple; he knocked the man to the ground, and the fight broke out. They were six of the Miami crew and six of the Daniels crew. Two other pistols were pulled by the Miami group, and one went off, but nobody was hit. All the guns were taken from the Miami group, and let's just say the shit hit the fan, and the Daniels family went to a gunfight with their fists, and they beat the hell out of them and sent a message back to their organization.

The Miami group came to their senses, and they bought the marijuana back and then hired the Daniels crew to start working for them since they were the best of the area. The moral to this short story is this: this was the only family ever known or been around that went to a gunfight and the guns were thrown down and their fists were used and as they beat the shit out of these guys and they crawled back to their cars and got the hell out of there.

CHAPTER NINETEEN

Helping Each Other Out

As the jobs progressed, the law got tighter and tighter in the area. It was a known fact that the other local crews would help each other out from time to time when needed. There were three crews that worked in this area. The Weeks crew, the Totch Brown crew, and the Daniels crew. When larger jobs came ashore, and one crew could not handle the whole job, then another crew would step up and help out. The Daniels crew had the largest crew of all and had worked in the area the longest.

The Daniels crew was also working for Larry. Larry had the park rangers bought and in their back pockets. It was great to work for someone with this kind of power. With this kind of power came with a lot of privileges.

Larry was also the watch boat for the Daniels crew when they were doing certain jobs. Watch boats were used to watch the waterway and make sure no one was approaching or surprising them while they were moving the marijuana. Larry was also used by the marine patrol (FWC) to tag fish in the national park and release back into the water at the same time he was watching, so if someone who caught the fish could report back as to the condition of the fish and where it was caught back to the government recordings.

Suspicion arose when the Daniels crew noticed that Larry was working with the head marine patrol agent supposedly tagging fish. The crew now wondered if the fish they were tagging was the Daniels crew itself, all in all, and they just used the fish tag as a cover story so people didn't know what they were actually up to.

*****

About two weeks later, a friend of Kent's had bought a beautiful dog. It was a rottweiler to be specific. The dog was bought in Germany and flown over and delivered to the United States.

Once the dog landed in Miami, Kent went and picked him up at the airport. Kent put a rope around the dog and walked the dog through all of the perimeters of the yard. As he walked him around the yard, Kent would tell him "This is your yard," so the dog would be familiarized with everyone who lived there and with his surroundings, including the wraparound porch that dawned on his parent's house. He would stop by each window and tell the dog whose room it was and who would stay there.

Kent then opened the door and brought him through the house doing the same thing. He asked his mother to sit down in her chair where she normally sat. He walked the dog to mother, and Kent told the dog to take care of her and love her, and the dog took his paws and put them in her lap and then followed with putting his head in her lap. From that day forward, that was his mom's dog. The property was fenced, and Kent never kept the dog tied up.

After a few weeks, the dog started to become very protective of the family. If you came to the house and they said to come in, the dog was okay with that and never barked, but if you came up and put your hand on the door, the dog would go crazy barking.

The dog loved to ride in the truck with Kent, and he just loved to go, period. If Kent was going into Everglades City, he would take the dog along. Kent had always heard that dogs had a keen sense of a person, whether he was good or bad. For some reason, the dog would act differently with different uniformed officers, like if the county cop would approach the truck, the dog would lie down in the bed of the truck, and when he got closer, he would jump up and start barking at him and then stop, and it looked like the dog would start laughing at him. Then when a state trooper would approach, he would just raise hell and go crazy barking. The park ranger would get close to the boat or the house, and if Kent was in a store, he would have to run outside and catch the dog.

One day, the family was sitting around the table, and Randal said he wanted some mullet to fry up, and John wanted some to smoke for the family. Joe and Kent said they would go and get some. They headed out towards Gate Bay to go fishing. The boys found their mullet and caught about one hundred heads of the mullet, iced them down, and now they were on their way back. When they got into Chokoloskee Bay, and headed down towards the house, Joe looked at Kent and said, "We have blue lights behind us."

Kent replied, "Don't even look at them, and let's just act like we didn't see them."

Kent and Joe outran them the tied the boat up and put the mullet in the truck and took all of the fish over to John's house to clean and smoke all but the ones they were taking home to fry. Their dad was cooking the fish, and Kent and Joe were sitting at the kitchen table when Dad looked out the window and saw a marine patrol car pulling up and he said, "Wonder what the hell this is about."

Kent looked at his father and said, "That would be for me."

Randal looked at Kent and said, "What in the hell did you do?"

Kent replied, "I outran him."

So Kent opened the door and went out on the porch, and the patrolman, along with another man that was undercover with him, was standing on the bottom steps.

Mother had roses at either side of the entry of the steps. Kent told the officers to stay right where they were because he had a dog, and he would damn sure catch them.

"It is a Rottie."

Kent asked him, "What do you want."

The man responded, "I want to speak to you because you outran me."

Kent said, "Where in the hell were you, I had never seen you."

Walking down the stairs, Kent was looking for Yogi the dog. Yogi had already got wind of them being there, and he had walked over and was sniffing the clothes of the undercover man.

Kent told the man, "When I am running a boat, I look straight ahead at the speed I was running, where did you come from?"

The patrolman answered, "Sand-fly Pass."

Kent asked, "Did you put your siren on?"

The patrolman said no.

The patrolman asked Kent what he had on the boat.

Kent replied, "Mullet."

Yogi was standing and hiked his leg on the rose bush, and he never stopped hiking his leg, and Yogi took a step back on three legs and continued to pee, then the Patrolman stepped back, and Yogi stepped right with him with his leg still hiked on the patrolman, who had his pants tucked into his boots. On the third time, the undercover agent asked the marine patrol agent to stand still, and Yogi filled his boot completely with urine.

After Yogi finished, he scratched the ground and walked off. Randal, Kent, and Joe were dying laughing, and the undercover agent looked at the other man and said, "Come on, Pee-on, let's go." It was funny how a dog reacted to uniforms. This is the tale of how Yogi did not like men in uniform.

Even though Yogi was the great protector, he had a friend. Every evening, Yogi had a dolphin that would come up and play with him. The dolphin would splash his tail until he would get Yogi's attention, until he would come over and play. The dolphin would spit the water at Yogi and would even swim with him, and sometimes it would last fifteen to twenty minutes, and sometimes it would last an hour or so. The family always enjoyed sitting on the porch and watching Yogi play with his friend.

CHAPTER TWENTY

Introduction of the T-Craft

Today, the Daniels crew decided to graduate to using the T-Craft. This boat could haul more marijuana at any one given time. The first jobs were set to only carry four thousand pounds at a time, and now with the new boats, they could carry eight thousand pounds at a time, which was doubling the load and increasing their revenue substantially. Now with the larger loads, the trucks hauling the marijuana on land was to increase in size as well. Semi-trucks were required, and freezer trucks were used for the pot to be transported as well into the Miami area. Panel trucks and box trucks were used as well, as the dump trucks were still being used.

One of the first jobs that were done was a forty-thousand-pound job brought in by two crab boats into Plover Key. That night was a nice dark clear warm night, and the sky was as clear as could be, and the stars were shining bright. The water was as calm as glass, not even a ripple except for the fish jumping in the water, which looked like a ball in the water made from the phosphorous. When the fish would swim off, it would look like a trail that would glow a streak behind them. The crew was sitting there waiting for the boat to come in to offload. The guys enjoyed the light show the fish put on around the boat, and then they could hear the birds starting the sounds of the call of the wild as they started to roost on the nearby island, hunkering down for the night. Sitting around and everyone talking when they heard the all-too-familiar sound of the exhaust of the crab boats approaching. Now the crab boats were arriving to be offloaded into the eight t-craft and were set to set to bring the load into Chokoloskee Island. This particular job was a double job. The first two crab boats came in at nine o'clock. It was already decided on how it was going to be handled and where they were going to go with the load. Taking the watchers on to the boat and sending the crab boats back out into deeper water. Each boat carried approximately five thousand pounds. This would guarantee that the boats could get on top of the water without being overloaded with extra weight, and they could run at top speed. Remember, the new boats were now equipped with two engines instead of one.

On the way in, Kent brought the boat into the mouth of Fish Hawk Pass where Rutter Bar met up at the mouth. Kent was in the lead as he went down this tight narrow waterway, and Kent's mind wandered back in time. This was where he could imagine his grandfather would row his boat twelve miles through the passes on a low-rising tide to court his grandmother, fishing on the way over and staying a day or so, then returning on a high-falling tide to return home. And then he would think of his great grandfather poling the boat through the pass, and he was reminiscing how this would have been and what it would have been like. As the light cool spray of the water and the wind hit Kent in the face, he thought now he was running this new T-craft, and his ancestors could not even imagine the power these boats had. Kent was trying to see what it would have been like if his grandfather had this kind of power on a boat for him to use. It would have probably only taken twenty minutes or so.

Now the guys were running as they crossed the bay, so when they got close to land, they had to throttle down to an idle to keep the noise level low so they could come in undetectable.

The local townspeople all got in on the act. They used their vehicles that they could use for the hauling to make extra money. The local drivers were paid three dollars a pound. Which would be, on average, two thousand pounds a load, and the bigger truck could haul up to fifteen thousand pounds. As you can see and do the math, this was lucrative even for the locals that didn't go out on the water.

This job came off without a hitch, and the new boats proved to be worth their weight in gold, as they were faster and slicker in the water. But with new boats came new problems. The clan was running the boats at faster speeds, and the chase became more intensive, making this a much more dangerous job.

The second job was due to come in, and the instructions were given to ease their boats to the backside of Pavillion. With the faster boats, the Daniels crew could do two or three jobs a night, which meant high profits. For everyone. They now arrived, and they were sitting there waiting for another boat to get there, which was another forty thousand pounds, giving them a total of hauling eighty thousand pounds for the night.

As the guys were sitting around, they asked Kent, "I think this is the boat that you have a history with."

Kent replied, "What in the hell are you talking about?"

The crew then said, "This is the boat that had that little monkey that whipped your ass on it. Maybe they will have another one on the boat for you."

The crew started laughing and giving Kent a real hard time about the fight.

Kent then said, "There is no telling what they will have down below this time."

Kent reached over and grabbed the bottle of vodka and said, after taking a drink and chasing it with Coke, "You can bet your sweet ass I will not go below deck. I will not be the first one anyway."

They continued to wait on the boat *The Sally Ann*. The familiar sound of the boat started in a distance.

Kent asked, "Are we going to let them come into us, or are we going to run offshore to them."

"Yes, let's run offshore and meet them and get this over with."

The radio came on, and with a booming voice, Randal said, "I am firing Pompano."

The boat came back on and said, "I have my net back on the boat, and it's cleared."

"All right then, we are going to be heading your way."

"Okay, I'll put the coffee on."

All the boats started heading out to the *Sally Ann*. It was located a mile offshore. Getting to the boat, the crew jumped on the boat and started loading the T-Craft as quick as they could. Now that the boats were loaded. They never duplicated a job in the same place in one night because if one got busted, they didn't want to lose both. So they were on the move once again. They were taking this one to Plantation Island, and they wanted to make damn sure they got their money out of this job.

"Kent, we are going to put 6,500 pounds on the boat with you."

Kent replied, "Okay, not a problem." Kent then asked, "Where do you want me to take this to?"

They then told Kent they were going to put an extra man on the boat for him.

"And I am going to have two vans waiting for you right at the airport. Right by the rangers station."

This airport was designed for small aircraft only. Nothing too big could come in there.

Kent looked at him and said, "I hope you get this one taken care of."

Randal responded, "That's not something you have to worry about. Just don't make a lot of noise."

Kent was making his way to Sandfly Pass, and the others were going to Houston Bay and make their way to their destination on Plantation Island. As he got closer and coming to Sand Fly, he would go on the backside of it. He came out into the bay, and he would turn his motor off and listen for any other boats. He then started his boat up and eased his way across.

One of the crew then asked, "Are we really going to the park rangers station?"

Kent replied, "That is where we were told to go."

The crew member looked at Kent like he was crazy and said, "Okay then."

The number one crewman turned around and told Kent, "Let's do this."

Running the bow of the boat up in the grassy area, Kent eased the up to the end of the run strip. Kent stayed at the helm, and the crew started loading the vans. Kent, always being cautious, was watching out for the crew, making sure no one came upon them.

A telephone call came in, and all the captains were called to a meeting at the Oyster Bar Restaurant. Sitting around, they told them that they had a job coming in that night. They had been working steadily for thirty days straight, and there was a dance at the Golden Lion. It was Friday, and the wives said that if they and their husbands were not there for the dinner and dance, it was going be hell to pay.

Kent and Craig started laughing and cutting up when Darryl looked at them and said, "What in the hell is so funny?"

Kent turned around and had this grin on his face, and Randal replied, "Oh shit."

The guys said, "What did you say that for?"

Randal said, "Kent has something on his mind."

Kent replied, "Yes, I do."

Kent told Randal to give him three boats, and they would go out and get the job in daylight.

Kent then explained that "They never expect us at this time of day, we always work at night."

Craig said, "I'll go with you."

John said, "Me too."

Brent said, "You aren't leaving me out."

Because they would be talking about this for years.

Kent then asked, "Where was this job going to."

They replied, "Over at Freddie's landing, at the point."

They guys were talking that they were going to leave at Chokoloskee and to Turners River and go out to the point of the sand behind the trees. They were going to meet up there at five-thirty, and Kent then told the guys not to leave from the same place.

John said, "I will come out of Fish Hawk Pass."

Brett said he would go Lopez River to the secret creek.

Craig said he would go north and come out behind Red Fish Key to Chokoloskee Pass.

Everybody met up at five-thirty, and everything was all set up because they had already made contact with the boat offshore. When the boat got within five miles, he was going to call them on the radio, and the guys were going to run to them. They met the boat and got it unloaded, and everything went well, so the guys went home, took a shower, and cleaned up, and were sitting at the dance by nine o'clock that night with their first drinks in their hands.

The rest of the crew asked, "How did things go?"

Kent replied, "I am here, aren't I?"

*****

That was one for the history books because it was unheard of to do these jobs during the daylight hours. As far as they know, the Daniels crew was the only one to have done a complete job during daylight, and with the marijuana sitting on the deck of the boat, and coming home to tell the tale.

CHAPTER TWENTY-ONE

Airboat Country

It was a hot and humid night, and there was no breeze around at all, and while the crew was sitting and waiting for the job to get started, the mosquitoes were eating them alive. Sitting there with the motors off and waiting to get the boats roaring to get the job going, you could hear the male alligator bellowing, frogs croaking, and the birds screeching off in the distance, letting you know you are sitting in the Everglades.

Today a big job with about thirty thousand pounds on it was coming into the area. The whole islands of Chokoloskee and Everglades City were hot as hell and crawling with law enforcement. The Daniels crew knew they were being watched, and they knew they had to get the job stashed into a brown-colored house located on Chokoloskee Island that was facing Turners River. Word got out quickly. The Daniels crew was a creative group and would pull out all stops to get their job ashore and get it sent to the warehouse where the head people were and could take care of the load and get it processed so they could be paid for the job. Since the law had already found out about this job, the Daniels crew kept all the information to themselves to make sure they could secure it in.

One of the local law enforcement officers caught wind of them watching the Daniels crew. Let's just say this man was a true friend, and he then sent a message to the Daniels crew, letting them know they were being watched, and trust me, he was paid very well for the information he provided.

The Daniels crew took the marijuana ashore and placed it in the garage of the house. This house was up on stilts because the area was prone to flooding. In the cover of the night, the following evening, the Daniels crew had a small window of opportunity to move the marijuana and get it out of there safely. They had to be inventive and were a little uneasy with this job because they had never used airboats or this method before, so until they saw how smooth it went, they had no idea about how much safer and easier it was to run a load like this out.

They picked up the job, and they took it through the Houston Bay heading to Turners River. Turners River ran from Chokoloskee Bay to US 41 and all the way to the north of Ochopee. Going up Turners River until they hit Two Palm Bay. Two boats were sent up at a time in this narrow waterway because this creek, which only had room for the boats themselves with no room to turn around in, was not wide enough for other boats to pass. They ran this area until they got to a body of water with sawgrass all around it. Then they would run the T-Craft boats aground. When these two boats would return, then they would send the next two and the next two until it was completed and all the marijuana was loaded into the airboats and they were on the last leg of the journey out of the Everglades.

When they got a mile and a half from highway from highway 41, they had two brothers in their airboats, both were twenty-foot long boats waiting on them. Only three thousand pounds could be loaded into each airboat at any one given time. The airboats only took ten minutes to run to the specific spot and then would run back and forth until all of the marijuana was all taken to the required destination.

This part of the park was known as an airboat country. Skimming through the Everglades on an airboat was a thrilling adventure even if you were hauling marijuana through the area. People were used to hearing the airboats running in this part of the country at high rates of speed all the time. People would hunt, go frogging, and travel through this thick sawgrass that was like a knife cutting through soft butter, and this was their playground. To protect the innocent, we are not going to name who were driving the airboats, but we are going to finish telling the story about this job.

This job was taken to Donna Drive to the public airboat landing. All the marijuana was offloaded into vans and box trucks. Now the crew had to hurry up and wait to make sure all of their trucks arrived safely, and all vehicles were taken into the drop-off spot in Homestead for a job well done. Money was collected, and the group returned to the Glades exhausted, worn out, and stressed to the max, and not happy about the pressure these two jobs put on them. This job was more tedious than others in the past. Other crews were less and less with the law tightening down on the illegal marijuana trade that had been exposed here. This crew was still hauling and were having to cover two and three jobs a night.

CHAPTER TWENTY-TWO

The Ghost People

This night started out like any other night. They were meeting the *Popeye*, and it was holding thirty thousand pounds on board. This job would take seven boats to get marijuana ashore. They got to the Pavilion and Little Pavilion; it was a calm quiet night but very dark, and the wind was a little chilly but nice. They started hearing the familiar sound of the *Popeye's* bubbling exhaust in the water, and they knew the boat was getting closer and closer. When the radio call came in, they made contact, and the crew sent a boat out to the *Popeye* to bring her in to where they were sitting waiting to offload her.

They would be listening for the different sounds of the exhaust on the boat to determine how far out she was. The Daniels crew could distinguish between the different exhaust sounds by the noise coming up deeper and heavier. A loaded boat sounded one way with the weight on her, but a lighter boat would sound completely different.

Getting the boat into position, the crew would throw the anchor of the *Popeye*, getting her ready to be offloaded. Once they started to unload the boat, Craig walked forward to the wheelhouse and looked at the radar. He noticed some spots that were being picked up on it that he didn't know what they were. Craig came out and looked for Kent, knowing that he knew the radar pretty well, and asked him if the spots were birds.

When Kent looked at the radar, he responded no, those were other boats, and they had them surrounded. "We have bigger boats

105

and smaller boats surrounding us, we have to get this shit off of here now."

The coast guard had seen the boat coming in from offshore, and the crew of the *Popeye* probably was not paying attention and let the boats get about five miles offshore from them, and they were being very careful not to be detected or make any noise. The Daniels crew could not hear them. Kent came out of the cabin and looked at Darrel and Randal and told them they had them surrounded and they need to get this shit offloaded real quickly.

Darrel said, "What the hell are you talking about?"

Kent replied, "Go look at the radar."

When Darrel came out, he yelled, "Let's get this shit unloaded, and everyone put all hands on deck and get her done." With about ten minutes to spare, the coast guard was about three-quarters of a mile away idling, trying to creep up on them. Everyone with the T-Craft and the *Popeye* was moving. Everyone, including the *Popeye* crew was, moved on to on the smaller T-Craft boats. They left no one behind. Kent had both of his motors running, and the crew had him untied. They were a minute away from being busted. Dwain tried to start his motors and flooded his engines.

Dwain yelled, "Kent, don't you leave me."

So the crew grabbed a rope and tied Dwain to Kent's boat, and Kent took off. Kent told Dwain to put the boat in gear and told his crew that when they saw the boat jump, cut the line and then told Dwain to turn away and don't run over the top of them.

In order to not make white water, they had to be careful to stay in between the *Popeye* and the beach so the radar could not detect them. White water was a foaming trail that a boat put off when it ran at a high rate of speed, and it took several minutes for it to go away. They could not determine between them or the beach. Once they got to the side of Pavilion Beach, they could get the boats on top and run wide open. Now they cut in the shore of the Pavilion and in between the two sisters and coming out of duck rock. They got there, and they headed over to Joes Camp Key. Looking offshore, you could see the coast guard boats put spotlights on the *Popeye*. So they had made it to them, and the *Popeye* was being boarded.

The coast guard looked around and put officers on board, and there were no people or marijuana on board this boat, and that pissed them off even more. The coast guard said there was no way this could have happened and that they must have been ghost people who have done this. There was no way anyone else could have gotten on the boat and unloaded it and then disappeared that fast.

They took the bales and hid them up in Gator Creek and headed in from a little scary night, which turned out to be easier than they had thought. After the job was finished, the crew headed out for some cool ones to wash down the salty sea air that accumulated in their throats.

CHAPTER TWENTY-THREE

The Scariest Job Ever

This was the worst trip Kent had ever had to do. It was the scariest one of all being chased by the law. Going out and coming back into port, Kent was at the *Bluebird* and at the helm, taking her across the gap and heading to Bogotá, Colombia.

When he arrived, he had fifteen thousand pounds he had to pick up. When he hit the port, Kent had a note that had a word on it, and he then gave it to a dockhand. They told him where to go and what time he could be loaded. The next morning after, it was loaded, and Kent and the crew took off heading back to the United States.

About two days into the trip on the route back home, the *Bluebird* got jumped by the law and was chased. The *Bluebird* had no choice but to take refuge in Mexican waters. Kent kept the boat right on the line so if the Mexican law came after them, they could go on another side; they were in international waters either way to make a run on either side. Every time they moved, the law enforcement moved. The *Bluebird* was an extremely fast boat and could run up to forty-two miles an hour.

Just left of Mexican waters, Kent told his crew to get the Bowie ready with the metal reflectors attached so when they threw them in the water, it would confuse the radar. They could not distinguish between the Bowie and a boat on the radar. When the law started chasing them, they ran to the Bowie instead of the bluebird. That was his opportunity to make a run for it. When Kent checked the radar, he saw heavy traffic in the Fort Meyers area and in the Everglades area, so he chose to turn and go towards the Keys. As he headed toward Bahia Honda Bridge, he raised the hydrofoils and sat the boat back down in the water and went right through.

When they got to the meeting point, they offloaded with no problem, and Kent back to the Bahia Honda area. He pulled the seacock and the boat would sink down into certain areas of the boat, and then they would pump the water out, cleaning all the areas and residue where the pot had been stacked. Then they headed back to Marathon where they stored and kept the boat.

On route back, the coast guard came upon them and blue lighted them. Kent stopped and look at them and asked, "Why are you stopping me?"

The coast guard said, "For drugs."

Kent replied, "There are no drugs on the boat and you are welcome to look."

Kent told them that the radar was out and they had gotten lost but finally made it back to an area that he recognized and came home.

The coast guard kept them out there for four hours looking through every nook and cranny on the boat and finally had to let them go.

When he got back, Kent went to collect for the job and was talking to the head of the Columbian organization. Kent was telling him how hard the job was and how they were chased the whole time and how they had to maneuver through areas that they normally didn't go through when the Columbian leader started laughing and said, "If they had stopped you, there were only five pounds of marijuana on the boat. The rest was coffee beans that we needed for a party we are having, so you see if you had got caught, it wouldn't have been with that much."

The Colombian leader then asked, "Didn't you look at the numbers on the side of the bales?"

Kent replied, "Yes, I did."

"Then you should have noticed that the numbers were different. That is the way we can distinguish between what we have coming in when we stack it."

Kent then said, "That was coffee?"

"Yes, it was."

Then Kent looked at the man and said, "I really don't care because it pays the same."

The man responded, "Yes, it does."

CHAPTER TWENTY-FOUR

Young Boy in Trouble

They had a job on the other side of Plover Key, and they were running down to meet the boat. On the way down, Randal saw a blinking light doing an "SOS" on Pavilion Key. He knew something was wrong, and he felt someone was in trouble, so he had to go see.

When he pulled up to the beach, there was a young family and a young boy which had canoed down to the desired island. Their son was running down the beach and had stepped on a horseshoe crab, and the barb had gone all the way through his foot. Which was very painful. When Randal saw the boy, he knew he needed medical attention as soon as he could get him there.

Randal called the boat he was meeting and told them he would be a few hours late because this family was out on Pavilion in a canoe with his family and was pretty seriously injured and had to be taken to the hospital. Randal decided to take the family into his home, where he could get his wife, Joyce, to take them to the hospital.

When he arrived at the home, he had to explain to Joyce what had happened, and he told her to take them to the hospital and stay with them until they were finished because they had no ride back to the area. Which she did. The boy and his family arrived within fifteen to twenty minutes of Randal picking them up on the beach, and then Joyce rushed them to the hospital.

After Randal got out to the larger boat, it was already in the process of being offloaded. Instead of bringing the job in, they placed the marijuana up a creek and placed it in the woods in the roots of the mangrove and hid it. The reason they did this is that they did not know if Randal had triggered the marine patrol to be looking for them or not, so to be safe, this was what they did to protect the job.

The next night, once they figured out that it wasn't hot, they moved the marijuana bales to their standby trucks and routes to move the marijuana into the Homestead area.

CHAPTER TWENTY-FIVE

Floyd and the Monkey

Floyd was sent to Colombia on a shrimp boat to pick up approximately twenty thousand pounds. Down in the South American countries, Floyd was a man who was well-respected and liked by many.

Floyd was known to be the only man to have been incarcerated in seven different countries and could talk his way out of trouble for himself and his crew. Floyd was always called in to help others that were detained in these countries when no one else could help.

On the trip, Floyd went down to get the marijuana, and that was when they would send a Columbian back with the job to the United States. They were put there to watch the job from start to finish. These people were never paid that much money, so to augment their money, they would bring different animals into the United States sell on the side. On this particular job, they brought a young chimp, and on the way back across, Floyd had noticed the monkey in the cage. Floyd became infatuated with the monkey and would play with him, so Floyd brought the monkey out of the cage up to the wheelhouse, where he was at the helm of the boat, to be with him. Floyd would let the monkey sit in his lap and drink beer. The monkey soon learned to drink beer with him, and soon the monkey and he became good friends. The monkey would play around on the floor and on the wheel out of the age.

When Floyd got close to where the drop-off point was and the night ahead of schedule, Floyd made a little better time than he thought he was going to. He stayed offshore in about fifty to sixty feet of water. While sitting there, another job was scheduled to come in. It was a known fact that if you were scheduled for a particular night, that was the night you got worked or they would have to hand the job off to someone else.

That night Floyd was sitting there, and he realized on the radar that coast guard was moving towards him. Floyd became a little concerned and was running from the coast guard and moved the boat a little closer to shore, and in the process of moving away from the coast guard, he ran the shrimp boat aground on the edge of the mangroves and gave the order for everybody to leave the boat. Everyone was starting to jump off the bow of the boat, even Floyd. When Floyd realized he left his little buddy back on the boat, he went back to the boat and climbed up and brought his friend to the bow and then threw his little buddy on the soft sand of the mangroves. Floyd then jumped off the boat again and hit the sand. When he hit the sand, he twisted his ankle and broke it. Unable to run, he sat down and just waited for the coast guard. As the story goes, when the coast guard showed up and Floyd and the monkey were sitting on mangroves edge, with guns drawn, the monkey was pointed fingers at Floyd as to say he did it.

Now with Floyd being busted, the Daniels crew was unaware of what was going on. The coast guard and The Marine patrol figured that Floyd was going into Everglades City. They knew the Daniels crew went out and was waiting for the other job. By the time they got the big boat unloaded, they had called the coast guard and the marine patrol, and they knew the crew was out there. They would run their boats, and then they would cut the engines and listen for any movement or sound from other boats. They were out there next to the Gulf of Mexico and back in this time period, only had a two-stroke engine, so when it was opened up, it was very loud, and the other sound was the water hitting the bottom of the boat.

They had the other job come in around nine o'clock that night. They got everything off the boat. There were six of them. While they were offloading the big boat, the captain came to the back of the boat and announced that Floyd from the other job was busted. He had heard it on the radio, and you could turn it to channel sixteen and monitor it. The Daniels crew really didn't think much of it.

On the way in somewhere around Lumbar Key, all hell broke loose. Blue lights came out of nowhere, and the boat came out of everywhere. Now it was every man for himself, and everyone was running trying to get away from the law.

Kent was one of the last boats heading in. The other boats were a quarter of a mile or so ahead of them. He slowed the boat down and told the crew, "We are going to have some fun tonight."

The crew responded, "Do you want us to throw it?"

Kent replied, "No."

As he lit up a cigarette and reaching under the console of the boat for his liquid courage and took a big drink of vodka, he asked the crew if they wanted some.

The crew asked, "What are you going to do?"

Kent said, "I am going to join the chase. They are expecting us to go south, and I am going north." He could still see boats and blue lights ahead of them. He remarked it looked like a bunch of fireflies out over the dark water. Kent figured he could get to an area that had mangroves. He could offload the marijuana in the woods and hide it and go ashore. They would at least have enough money to pay the crew.

Kent stayed offshore and headed north. Got up off Stop Key on the other side of the Indian Key channel, turning back into the mangroves to Stephens Pass and was heading Feckahatche Bay. He figured he would take it up to Gasoline Alley, which had a tight narrow gap. He had to come through with mangroves on both sides. When he came through the hitching post on the other side, there were two boats waiting that fell in behind him. Ahead of him was another gap; he had to make a sharp left and a sharp right, and there was a mangrove island. He made the left, but when he made the right, he didn't make it and went through the island. When he came out the other side, the tide was about three quarters and rising, and he knew if he got to open water, he could outrun them. He turned and went through bright mullet pass. There were a lot of oyster bars and twist and turns. Coming out of the pass, he made a sharp left to Russel Pass.

Whenever you are running sixty miles an hour or better, Kent was gaining ground and losing the law. Coming out of her and into a place that had a little shell island, they slid into a creek behind it and quickly unloaded the 3,500 pounds they had on the boat. Coming back out, Kent shut his motor off so he could hear where the other boats were. He turned back toward the sound of the boats and headed back. Because he didn't want them to find where he hid the stuff. So they ran back toward the noise, and when he hit Indian key pass, they saw him; they saw the spray just like they saw his. Not knowing if the rest of the boats made it, he didn't want the law going back into that area. So he then ran offshore and headed south like he was going to the Florida Keys. About five miles offshore he cut the engine and told the boys there is no noise so let's wash the boat and get all the residue out. Kent then eased the boat in and went back to Chokoloskee Bay and they would cut the engines and listen and then run again if there was no noise until they came ashore and tied up to the dock. Out of the six boats, only three made it ashore with their load, and Kent was one of them.

CHAPTER TWENTY-SIX

The Mariel Boatlift

The first time he went down to the Mariel Boat Lift, he went on a boat called the *Sharon and Daren*. He would pick up on the side of the mountains where the cliffs were to pick up the people. According to the Lorene and the compass and charts, they would wait and blink lights at them, and the people would come out. It would be the damnedest things that these people would come to the big boat to board. They never took them back to the port where they docked the boat. Sometimes smaller boats would come out and meet them and get the people they were carrying. When they got finished dropping the people, they would get down to the dock and scrub the boat down with bleach all over it. Most times they used the same crew that they fished with. This was to ensure the safety of the crew to make sure they didn't bring anything back unknowing to them.

When they would come back across, they would keep the people hidden in the bottom cabin and not on the deck. They never tried to carry more than twelve people at a time. That was all they were being paid for. He went to Cuba two or three times with the same boat picking up people. These people left their life behind them just to leave Cuba. A very small amount of mementos but nothing too much. It always amazed Kent because he didn't understand how Cuba was and how people could leave their life until Kent started looking into it.

Most of these people lived in shacks, and others were from very wealthy families. Once Kent got the bluebird, he had a friend with the last name of Papa Patiesta. Papa was the elder of the family, and Kent knew him for three to four years, and they called his wife Mama Patiesta. They were very good people and spoke little English. They could communicate the proper Spanish and could be understood if spoken slow and distinctive. They had a harder time understanding Kent because he was influenced by TV and other things, making his language more slang, but they could understand him, with his southern country accent.

Kent was talking to Papa and Mama Patiesta one day, and the boat lift came into the topic of conversation. Castro had it set up where you could come into port, and Mr. and Mrs. Patiesta asked Kent to go get their family.

Kent went to Cuba, and he had to pull into another port. This was where all the news crews and other people were going. When he pulled into the port, he pulled between two cliffs, and they eased off the throttle, and they were not the only boat there. As they got closer, there was a concrete dock about one thousand feet long and had three finger piers coming off the dock. Kent eased up to the pier, and some of the military people came out and met the boat. Kent handed the man a paper that showed the names of the people he was picking up. He then told Kent to back away from the dock, and they would call him up to pick them up once they had the family ready. This could take a day or so since there was paperwork that had to be done.

Once anchored Kent looked back towards the cliffs; he noticed facing out on the right-hand side that there was a levee, and it had a concrete deck on it, and sitting on that was a bulldozer with no blade on the front. And hooked to the end of it was a chain that was the links that were eight inches long, a ship anchor chain, not a small one, a very large one. The chain went down from the dozer to the water, and at night, they would lift that chain out of the water and block off the area so no one could get into that port. The next morning, they would back the dozer up and drop the chain back down in the water and allow the boats to come in and out of the port. Keep in mind, this dozer was not new; it was very old, and it took a while to get her started so they could mover her.

The next day around 9:00 AM, they motioned to Kent on a bull-horn, and they announced that they would be taken next, and they would be taking prisoners back with them and not the people they had come to get. Kent told them he was only there to get the Patiesta family and no one else, and if not, he would leave. They replied they would blow him out of the water and sink the boat before they left. Which naturally then everything was fine, and he would carry the prisoners.

Kent already had the engines running, recharging the batteries on the boat. He was ready to go. Kent and the crew were sitting there talking and taken their shirt off and left their shorts on like they were sunning. Kent had an anchor hole, and this was where when you pilled the anchor, and if water went in, it would keep the water from coming in the cabin. Kent told Jonny to lay out like he was tanning, and when he felt the anchor line pull tight, to cut the anchor rope and to roll in the anchor hole, and then they were leaving. When the line came off, he cut the line, and Kent threw both throttles wide open. Kent had been to diesel engines screaming, and then he lowered the hydrofoil so he could make this boat go forty-two miles an hour running light. Being careful, he had to raise the front first and then not to raise the back too much because if he did, the prop would take air. He would be dead in the water at the Cuban government's mercy.

Now in front of them was the bulldozer with the chain, and now they were starting the dozer, and Kent could see the black exhaust coming out of her, and the only thing at this point he was praying for was they did not get that chain taut before he got the boat on the other side of it. They had a little wooden twenty-foot boat that had a diesel engine in it. It didn't move fast, just about fifteen miles an hour. It wasn't a problem to outrun her, but he couldn't outrun the machine guns that were mounted on the back of the boat and the two guys holding additional machine guns in their hands. When they started shooting at the boat, they never shot below the waterline. He came through the cliffs and into about eight-foot seas heading to international waters.

Kent had eight miles to get out of Cuban waters. About the time they hit international waters, this jet came over the top of the boat that he believed to be a Russian MIG. Reaching for his VHF mike, he called the coast guard and was informed they could not get to him for forty-five minutes because they were too far away. Another call came in and asked what their problem was. Kent replied that he was Captain Kent Daniels and was a flagship of the United States and he had a Mig all over him. He informed him he was a minute away from him and would be assisting him. He asked what his documentation numbers were on the boat, and Kent had them painted on the top for easy view, and since this was a net fishing boat, he had to have the bowie color of the boat and the net numbers "X1317" white bottom and red top. And the crawfish bowie color was the same thing the crawfish number was X3510.

About thirty seconds later, this jet dropped down in front of him and turned up and sprayed a rooster tail a hundred feet in the air and a hundred feet long. He then asked Kent if that was him and told him, "You are running along with the good." Whenever he pulled up, he got behind the other aircraft. The radio that he had that had chips in it allowed them to hear other frequencies. These were called two-way radios, and they were only used in emergencies. He came on and said he was United States Air Force, and he was pursuing a United States flagship and wanted to know their intentions.

With no reply, again, he repeated, "I am a lieutenant colonel of the United States Air Force, what are your intentions?

At this point, Kent had realized he had a pain going through his left leg, and he touched his leg and could feel a burning sensation and could smell flesh burning, and he realized he was bleeding. Another radio call came on and said simply, "I have you locked what is your intention."

Kent looked at his crew and said, "Boys, I have been shot."

The crew replied and said, "Where?"

Another radio call came over and said, *Bluebird*, you are clear."

Then another call came in from the coast guard and said, "*Bluebird*, I need to see you in Key West."

Kent responded, "I would be heading that way." And he never told them he was shot. Before you went down to pick up anyone Cuba, you were supposed to go by Key West and let them know.

"Boys, you are going to sear the hole shut and stop the bleeding." The most pain Kent had ever felt was when the alcohol hit the wound and stopped the bleeding. Kent sat there and had a few drinks to ease the pain. He then tied the boat up to the dock and layed all of the paperwork on the dash to be inspected. He then instructed the crew not to tell the Coast Guard he was shot. He then explained to get ready they are going to go over the boat with a white glove and inspect it." Kent then instructed the crew. When they ask what they were doing in Cuba, tell them we were there to pick up some people, and when they wanted to put prisoners on the boat and Kent refused them, they shot him.

They cleaned that boat up, spotless, and he went ahead and dropped the boat down and was a regular boat. They got there and got tied up and went through the boat with a fine-tooth comb, and the crew had all the paperwork for the boat. They sat there and said, "Captain, do you realize that they honeycombed the ass end of your boat. The only thing they could have thought of, they were trying to shoot the motors of your boat." After a couple of hours and a good lecture about picking up anything from Cuba, they released them, and they went back to Marathon. Yes, the Patiesta family was finally picked up, and he didn't go into port, and they came out to the boat one way or another, and yes, they arrived in the United States in good condition.

CHAPTER TWENTY-SEVEN

The Rookery

Randal, Darryl, Craig, and Paul were out one night and went to shoot a rookery and got some birds to eat. While they were shooting the Rookery with the guns going off, the marine patrol heard the guns being fired. The marine Patrol headed into Pumpkin Key. He saw Darryl and the others picking up the birds that they have shot and fell in the water.

When the man came up and blue-lighted Darryl, he started talking to the marine patrol. Darryl called Bobby out, and Randal told him not to say a word, and he swam to the boat to keep everyone else from being busted. Randal told Bobby that they would get him out as soon as they left there.

Kent was sitting in the Golden Lion drinking when everyone left halfway drunk. Kent headed home and Aunt Sue called him to get him to get home quick. Kent looked at his cousin Clay and said, "You got to go help me out."

Kent went to his mom and dad's house and told his mother to give him the liquor and the soda pops, four quarts of vodka, and a case of Coke, with some beer as well. Going down to the rookery, they had to go through Chokoloskee Bay, and they had to go through a tight narrow gap, and on each side of this gap were two boats. Knowing that they were park rangers and marine patrol and knowing they were waiting for someone to go down to Pumpkin Key to pick the other guys up, and Pumpkin Key was out of the park, so the rangers had no jurisdiction.

Kent started to tilt his motor up and opened the motors wide open. Making about sixty miles an hour. The T-Craft had no seats. He looked forward and told Clay to sit down on the bottom of the boat and hang on. The closer he got, he could see that the gap was blocked off, and the two boats decided to get the hell out of Kent's way. When they moved out of the way, he shot straight through the bay they were trying to block, then Fakahatchee, and he was about five miles from Pumpkin Key. When you came through the hitching post, you were out of the national park. When he got to Santina Bay, he slowed and shut the motors off, reached in the cooler, and drank a big couple of gulps of vodka and gave Clay a beer.

He looked at Clay and said, "Let's go get our people."

Entering Monkey Key Bay, and the rookery sat across the bay. With somewhat of an Indian yell, he called his other family out. The yell was a yell that among the Daniels family they knew without saying a word.

Randal had around ten thousand in cash, and he stashed it in a tree so he wouldn't be caught with it. Kent asked his dad, "Do you want to take the helm?

Randal asked, "Not unless you have some vodka."

And Kent said, "Look in the cooler."

Randal took two big hits off it, and Kent told him he could not go out the way they had come in because there were two boats waiting, but this was the Ten Thousand Island, and there were many ways to get home other than the way they came.

They came on in, and the party was over. All arrived safe and sound. A couple of days later, Randal went to go get the money that he had hidden in the tree before they came back to the house. There he learned that a family of raccoons had torn it all up and had made them a very expensive nest to have their babies in.

Randal replied, "That racoon has some very expensive taste."

CHAPTER TWENTY-EIGHT

Boys Being Boys

After one of the big jobs that had come in, the boys decided to blow off some steam and let their hair down. Kent and Craig decided to go to the Captain's Table Chickie Bar and had a couple of drinks. They had only been there for thirty to forty minutes when Craig looked at him and said, "You know, we need to be in an airplane."

Kent said, "Where do you want to go?"

Craig responded, "Just up."

Craig had felt he wanted to take the piper cub up one of the planes we bought, so they got in Kent's truck and headed to the airport.

Once they arrived at the airport, Craig went to the front of the plane to hand prop and start the plane while Kent was in one of the seats of the cockpit. Kent had primed the engine and held the brakes and checked the plane out before take-off; Craig started the motor. Craig climbed in the back seat of the plane. The airplane could be controlled and steered by the stick of the airplane. Controls were in both seats, so either one could fly the plane.

They taxied down the to the run strip and took off into the wind, blowing about twenty-five miles an hour, which gave them a side wind. When they were taking off, they had to hold a hard right to keep themselves out of the trees. After they took off, they had to gain airspeed by staying close to the water so they could lift once they gained it.

After they reached their airspeed, they started climbing until they reach 300 to 400 feet, then they started monkeying around till they got to 1,500 feet.

Craig looked at Kent and said, "I want to loop the plane."

Once they got between 1,500 and 2,000 feet, Craig dropped the nose and started falling to get airspeed. Three hundred feet from the water, he pulled up and started making the loop.

Kent looked at him and said, "I want to hammerhead the plane."

So they climbed back to two thousand feet and had the plane sticking straight up and down, and once they got to three thousand feet, the plane could not go any further; the plane would stall and fall back. After about fifteen more minutes of playing around, Craig and Kent decided to buzz the Chickie Bar.

Kent decided he wanted to touch the wheels on the water and pull the plane back up. They did so. Leaving that area and flying right by the Everglades Bridge and following the canal around, they got into where it opened up into a small bay and where the bridge crossed it. Kent flew around the small island that was on the side of the bridge. He then proceeded to make a hard left bank towards the bridge with the wings straight up and down When he got to the bridge, he flattened his wings out and flew between the bridge and the powerlines, flying right on the water until they got to Dupont.

Craig looked at Kent and said, "Let's go have a drink at the Port of Islands." And he took the helm back from Kent. On the way there, they would always fly the parries, and they found a couple of deer they could chase and found a bear to look at, then they went on over to the islands. Sitting there at the bar, having a good time, laughing and joking, and having a good time because they were considered the life of the party. All the barmaids were always glad to see them.

After having two drinks apiece, they decided to leave and left a one-hundred-dollar bill on the bar for the service, because they would leave large tips. After, they made their way to the airport and took off, landed, and took Kent's truck back to the Chickie Bar. Upon arrival, there was no one there, and Kent said, "Craig, no one is, here everyone left."

Craig said, "As long as we have a bartender, we can drink by ourselves."

They walked inside the bar and noticed the bartender was crying. When she looked up and saw them, she thought she had seen a ghost. Craig asked where was everyone.

"The bridge," Lori was shaking. "You guys are dead, you hit the water trying to fly under the bridge." Still crying, Lori said, "You guys are dead."

And Craig said, "We are right here, Lori. We are not dead."

Then Kent replied, "Then give the dead men a drink." Kent could not convince Lori that they were alive, and finally grabbing her hand and touching her, she realized they were alive.

"What in the hell is going on here? You crashed, and the fire department was dragging the bay for your bodies."

Craig and Kent thought it was a joke. Sitting at the end of the bar, still laughing, the boys looked up and saw their mother and father walking in the bar. They had come into talk to Lori to see what they had been doing right before they had crashed and died. Randal stood between the boys, and Joyce stood on the other side of Kent.

Randal looked up and said, "Y'all aren't fucking dead."

Kent replied, "No, we ain't dead."

And with the way Randal spoke with his left hand and his finger bouncing up and down, Randal said, with his slow southern drawl, "You are going to be in just about five Goddamn minutes."

Joyce didn't have to say a word. She said everything she needed to say with her eyes.

They turned around and left. That was the third time Randal and Joyce had a phone call that Kent was dead.

Then the next day, Craig and Kent were back up in Craig's plane, the underwing Comanche. The guys were doing their normal shit, flying around and trying to find what they could get into next. They left Everglades City and flew out toward Wootens, and they wanted to fly over the prairies and see how many deer they could see. Looking up, Kent saw the airboat that had gathered ahead of them.

Not knowing who was on the airboats, Kent said, "Let me have the control."

And Craig asked, "What are you getting ready to do?"

Kent replied, "I am going to scare the hell out of them." Kent took the helm, and they were about three hundred feet up, and he dropped the nose of the plane and headed straight at the airboat group of five. Kent pulled up and took his wing and hit the whip antenna on one of the airboats, and it was on the pilot side of the plane. He turned to come back; he looked down, and he saw, of all people, his mother standing on the platform of the boat right in front of her seat, shaking her finger at him. Kent looked at Craig and said, "In trouble again."

Craig said, "I bet your mama is proud of you now."

Kent said, "Yeah, you are sitting in the pilot seat, she didn't know I was flying."

CHAPTER TWENTY-NINE

New President with New Drug Campaign

New ball game. President Reagan was elected, and the new first lady had a slogan that read "Just Say No to Drugs." Ronald Reagan declared war on drugs and ordered the creation of the South Florida Drug Task Force. It was established to coordinate the efforts of various federal agencies that were now engaged with drug smugglers.

The government claimed that it was necessary to take down the drug lords. But its burden fell mostly on the people that were nonviolent marijuana users. The viewpoint was that the government finally had recognized what a huge problem drugs had become. Vice President Bush was in Miami, where he declared that major steps had been taken to stop the flow of marijuana that had been flowing into south Florida. President Regan even visited south Florida and had his picture taken standing in front of tons of marijuana that had been seized.

One late night, Vice President Bush, with his wife, were lying in bed when she was watching a local television broadcast interview with a red-headed young man, twenty-two years in age, standing on the docks in Everglades City, talking about the stone crab business and how it worked and how well the season was going, when he turned the conversation to smuggling marijuana through the Ten Thousand Islands, which surrounded the little village that they were talking about. The reporter was shocked when the young man started bragging to them about the amount of marijuana that was being brought in, and during his conversation, he told them that they were hugely successful because no one could catch them in the backcountry of the shallow waterways that only the local people knew how to maneuver so well.

Barbara Bush then woke the vice president up and explained that this young man made them look incompetent and "You need to get up and look at this." After watching the interview with his wife, it really infuriated the vice president because he felt as though they had made his campaign against drugs look terribly bad.

The following morning, he proceeded to tell his staff about the interview and to get that little town shut down. This was not acceptable, he explained.

Regan and Bush proclaimed their success in the war on drugs. They never mentioned that the price of marijuana was getting lower and lower, which meant that an abundance of marijuana flowing into the country was increasing. The war on drugs was a war on words, while the international trade of marijuana thrived. Regan declared the war on drugs to be one of his best achievements. Then the Iran-Contra scandal revealed that the US government had been trafficking in marijuana, as well as hard drugs, for military weapons. Many people did not understand what the Contra scandal was all about. It was really about oil and weapons and how Congress did not fund the money for the task force and other things they needed to keep the operation going.

Dating back to decades, the smugglers had been bringing in moonshine, rum, and cigarettes—just to name a few—into the unpatrollable maze of the waterway and mangrove islands along the southern coast called the Everglades. The hot commodity of the day was marijuana. Freighters from South and Central America would meet smaller boats from the area that would go out in the cover of the night and take on loads of bales of marijuana and bring them ashore.

The Daniels crew, being dubbed as the "Saltwater Cowboys" crews of local people from the Everglades area, were getting in on the action and earning thousands of dollars in a night's work. The activity was prevalent in the Chokoloskee Island and Everglades City area. This was where the young boys grew up on fishing boats that were as common as cars.

This area was a tight niche community where most people were related to each other, and outsiders were not trusted or welcome. The people not involved in the smuggling would not give any information on the ones doing it, making this one hell of a hard case to bust. No one down here would talk, so you couldn't prove anything.

In 1981, the first round of indictments came down in Operation Everglades One. Everybody in this small tight niche community who was hauling pot through the local waterways was now heading to jail. There were 125 people arrested that day and the weeks ahead. Boats used in the smuggling were seized and now was threating the economy of the tiny fishing village.

A year later, Operation Everglades Two came down yielding more arrests. Smaller investigations based on information on Operation Everglades One brought arrest into the late 1980s. Making the joke going around town that there were no men left here; they had all been arrested.

CHAPTER THIRTY

Operation Everglades One

Kent Daniels was loaded with fuel and supplies and headed back to Jamaica in the bluebird and was soon to be headed back with fifteen thousand pounds of marijuana under the deck. He was heading towards the Florida Keys and stayed offshore on the other side of Cuba. Remember, this was only a ninety-mile run to the Florida Keys. Kent had got a radio call and said that sharks were around their nets and fishing would not be good tonight.

Kent replied, "I will just stay at the house and see what would be good tomorrow night."

The next night, he received his call on the radio and was told the fishing was good and it was a bright beautiful night—in other words, *the coast was clear, let's bring it in.* So Kent fired the *Bluebird* up and ran like hell and brought the boat right on into Billy's place and had him place her in the cradle and take the props off, and Kent told Billy, by the way, she was fifteen thousand pounds heavier. Kent told him that the boat needed to look like he had the boat worked on for a couple of days. That was when Billy told Kent he could help him out but then asked if he had watched the news. Kent replied no, and Billy told him there was a big raid that took place in Everglades City and Chokoloskee, the Keys, and Naples.

Kent looked at him and asked, "Did you see my name on the news?"

Billy replied, "No, and I was looking."

Kent immediately returned to his house in Marathon and showered and then decided to call and see who had been arrested or who was on the run. Kent went back to Billy and told him that everything was fine, and he needed to have the props changed on the boat. Kent called home and told the crew, "I am going to need two vans to haul the props off the boat to Miami now as soon as you can. When the one van gets here, have them meet me at Castaways at noon for lunch."

The vans came and met Kent, and he sent them over to the boat on dry dock. He called Billy and told him that he needed him and his crew gone for a few hours. Billy did as he was asked, and they proceeded and loaded the vans and box trucks with the bales until every last one was out and finished and on its way out of the Keys, heading to homestead for their infamous drop. Upon completion, Kent stayed at the house for another day or two and then he loaded his stuff into the plane and flew home.

Upon arrival back in Everglades City, he asked around as to what had happened and triggered off the raid. Kent was concerned. He wanted to make sure nobody in his family had been picked up, and if they had, what were they charged with. To his surprise, no one in the family or crew were charged or arrested in this raid.

This was a little town that turned to drugs to augment their income after the government moved into the area and took away the locals' means of making a living to feed their families. Operation Everglades One came down, and 149 people were arrested. When the first arrest and the first indictments came into play, it changed everything. While the papers were being served and the handcuffs were placed on the men, doors were kicked down and men dragged out of bed, some with clothes and some without. Kids in beds, dogs outside were being shot and killed. All of this taking place in a small fishing village with less than six hundred people in the community of Everglades City, and it also flowed over into the Florida Keys, Miami, Naples, and the Fort Meyers area.

As the sunset and the clannish townspeople began the daily ritual of throwing down mug after mug of the ice-cold beer on tap that day, they rehashed their catch of the day or the long hours they had just spent in the Gulf of Mexico.

A slightly drunk ruddy-faced crabber, about twenty-five years of age, which most were very well built and cut with muscular forearms. Most of the crabbers are marked with the all too familiar scaring from the fiery stone crabs they work with. Then the story would turn from the angry stone crabs and the quest for their coveted claws to the evil that had plagued and altered the morals of the small fishing village located inside the Everglades National Park.

"Drugs have ruined this town," said the hard-bodied crabber in the sleeveless shirt as he drank down his beer and set the glass on the bar a little hard with frustration. Other people nodded their heads in agreement, but the men were not conveying discontent of the drugs that had entered the village.

They were saying that drugs had destroyed Everglades City for the simple reason that the people involved in the hauling of marijuana had been caught, and worse, with the clannish people, some were family, friends, and neighbors that remained silent when faced with the prosecution. Others turned on each other, which was the ultimate small-town sin! The money earned from the drugs helped the economy of the area flourish and provided things that the local townspeople could only dream about.

Everglades City was known as a beautiful unspoiled place and had one of the best fishing village that was ever known in the southern gateway to the Everglades National Park. A desolate area teeming with wildlife on the outer islands as well as the sawgrass marshlands.

On the morning of July 7, an armed convoy of more than two hundred drug agents and police swept into the tiny fishing village. They blocked off the only and the main road going into and out of the area and pulled off a major crackdown of the marijuana smugglers that lived in this town. The total number of people being arrested in this sting called Operation Everglades One climbed past three hundred, and 149 of them lived in Everglades City, nearby Chokoloskee Island and Copeland.

CHAPTER THIRTY-ONE

Gulf Pride Busted

This was December around the end of the month. Kent decided to go mullet fishing on the Gulf Pride and towed his mullet boat behind the bigger boat. They were going to meet two other boats in the area of Cape Sable around Sable Creek (The K Mail). They were heading to Ingram lake. Heading down it was going to be a three-hour run to get there before dark. They were going to meet up with other boats.

Kent had all of the supplies on that boat for a three- or four-night stay. With extra gas for the boats on board. On low tide, it was only a couple of hundred yards wide and a mile long down the center; it was very shallow, and you could run aground very easily. Cecil knew the area better than anybody. He was raised on Cape Sable as a kid.

Cecil on one boat and Dennis on the other, and the Gulf Pride was set up to take showers, eat, and lie down to sleep.

They made it down there, and they were sitting around talking. They had decided to take one boat at a time, and Cecil would be the best one to strike and rope the fish back on the boat and bring it to the Gulf Pride, where other guys were waiting to clear the net. Just for reference in this area, no fishing was allowed with nets. He kept doing this over and over, catching five to six thousand pounds at a time. When Cecil got the last boat back to the Gulf Pride, they got the nets back on the boat, and they iced the fish down. They had approximately eighteen thousand pounds in total. The next morning, the fish started moving north off Cape Sable, and there was about an acre of solid fish, which was in ten feet of water, making it easier for the boats to strike them. The next morning, up by daybreak, Cecil drank coffee, and Kent looked up and was watching the opening of the Sable Creek when the first fish started jumping.

Cecil said, "Let's get the crew up, we have about twenty minutes."

They sat around for the mullet to get right. They all agreed on how they were going to strike the fish. They would start out with two nets, with six hundred yards on each boat. They would get to the bunch of fish and run one way, and the other boat would run the opposite way, with the third boat running to the center, making a circle. There might be one hundred thousand pounds of fish in this school. But they could only catch a certain size fish that would be trapped in the four-inch gill net, so they only brought in about twenty thousand pounds. With three boats. They pulled the nets back on the boat and got them on the Gulf Pride and cleared the nets and iced them down on the big boat. It took about four hours to clear the nets, and they now realized that they did not have enough room in the iceboxes to take care of all the fish. The boxes held about five thousand apiece, and he only had three boxes.

Kent told Cecil that he was going to head to Islamorada in the Keys because it was closer to go there than to run back to the Everglades. The Islamorada fish docks were who had agreed to off-load the fish for them. They weighed the fish and gave them a ticket for their catch. The female was worth more than the male fish. They got them unloaded after icing them back up and fueling up, getting her anchored up and getting her in front of Sable Creek.

They decided that they were tired, and they were going to try to get some sleep for the night. The next day, getting up and moving around, everybody decided they were all hungry, and they all wanted to get something to eat. By the time breakfast was getting done, one of the crew members looked up and said, "Looks like there's a cloud in the water."

Cecil looked up and said, "Cloud my ass, that is fish."

They struck that bunch of fish and had about eighteen thousand pounds to this strike. They only used two boats this time. Clearing the fish and not wanting to take up the room in the cooler, and they threw the male fish on the deck and put the female on ice.

In a distance, Kent could see a couple of crab boats pulling their traps. "Cecil, look, there is a boat over there, and I am going to call them and see if they want to use these male fish for bait so that each boat took one thousand pounds." Word traveled fast around the crab fleet. The two crabbers told them to come back the next morning and take more off their hands. Each boat returned to the Gulf Pride and took two thousand pounds each. The crabbers asked if they could bring anything back for them.

Kent said, "Yes, I want some shrimp and crawfish, which is Florida lobster."

The crabber responded, "I will have them in the morning when I get back."

That night, Cecil did his magic trick again and would go on boat at a time strike, the fish, and bring them back to the Gulf Pride. Putting another fifteen thousand on the boat, leaving the male fish on the deck for the crabbers for the next morning, and the female on ice. The next morning, the first crab boat showed up, and they took two thousand pounds. Then the second crabber showed up and brought twenty pounds of shrimp and forty pounds of lobster and one thousand pounds of crushed ice. He had his crew shovel the ice onto the Gulf Pride, and he asked if he could take some home to eat. Kent said to "get all you want, just make sure you get the ones on ice so they are fresh."

Kent then asked, "Do you have any more boats coming?"

And they responded, "Oh yes, there is a couple more on their way."

Kent replied, "That's a good thing."

With the other boats showing up to get the fish off the deck of the boat, Cecil yelled, "There she jumped, you guys, better get ready. We only have about twenty minutes."

They fueled up the small boats. They sat and waited for the fish to get right, and when they struck, they caught thirty thousand pounds. Getting the fish back to the boat, and they were clearing the nets. This time when they finished, it was around three o'clock in the afternoon. They sat down and cooked a seafood buffet with all the different types of food there.

Kent looked at Cecil and said, "How much do you think we have on the boat?"

Cecil replied, "Thirty thousand pounds."

After the festivities of food and drink, they sat and talked and Kent said, "We need to get these to the dock."

Cecil replied, "Yes, I think we have had all the fun we can handle."

"Do you think the fish house can handle all of these fish?"

And Cecil said, "Not all of them, we are going to have to call all four."

They refueled the good boats back up so they could run back to Everglades city. He then told the other crew member to take his small boat so it would save some time by not pulling the boat behind them. Kent then cut straight across then cranked the boat up, getting her warmed up and getting the anchor pulled and heading on their way.

The crew asked, "Captain, do you need anything?"

He said, "Yeah, get me a drink and cigarettes up here, we are not going to run as fast as we could. I knew this was going to be a nice ride with the weather right." It was dark, and he was reaching up and turning his radar on making sure no other boats were in his path. All he was thinking about was getting to the docks. After two hours, Kent decided to slow the Gulf Pride down; he went to stretch his legs a little, walking outside the wheelhouse and checking everything out and making sure they weren't taking on any water and everything was still good.

Climbing on the side of the boat, Kent decided he needed to pee. Just about the time, he started peeing real good, the spotlight and the blue lights came on. Naturally, this was Coach Garden Park Rangers, and about the time they turned the lights on, Kent didn't see this coming. They hit Kent with the spotlight and asked him not to move. They came alongside the boat and told Kent to sit down on the engine box. Then he was asked what he was doing out there this time of night.

Kent looked at them and said, "I was heading to the dock."

And the ranger said, "What do you have onboard?"

Kent replied, "Fish."

The ranger said, "Fish or square grouper?"

Kent said, "Open the lid of the icebox."

And they could see the fish. They couldn't figure out how they had all those fish on board, and there was no net to be seen. They asked, "How did you have the fish?"

They asked Kent, "Where did you get the fish from?"

Kent said, "Out of the water."

Then Kent finally said, "We had three boats out there, and he was the head boat, hauling the fish in."

They asked who owned the boat. "Where is your paperwork?"

Kent told him that the boat belonged to them.

Finally the ranger came out and said, "He is clean, nothing on the boat."

Kent then told them, "I guess you want to harass everybody. You don't want anybody to make a living."

When one of the park rangers informed the coast guard that those people had to be careful of the people from the Everglades because they did not like law enforcement, Kent then informed the park ranger, "You are a damn liar."

They proceeded to let them go, and the coast guard looked at the rangers and said, "You may leave the boat, and Mr. Daniels, you have a safe trip back to the docks."

Getting back into the wheelhouse of the boat and heading on their way, the crew asked Kent and said, "Didn't the radar pick them up?"

Kent replied, "I wasn't paying attention."

Looking at him, he said, "Look, mix us a drink." And he turned the cabin light on and mixed the drinks.

Kent asked, "Reach on the bottom bunk in there and get me a package of the cigarettes I have down there."

He bent down and got the cigarettes. "And you are not going to believe this."

Kent said, "Yes?"

"Do you remember I told you I was going to bring some smoke with us? On the bunk, there was a quarter of a pound. And if they had found that, they would have taken the boat."

"We got away with this one."

"Barely."

This was what the people from Everglades or Chokoloskee had to put up with every time they went out on their boat, whether it was for pleasure or work. The people didn't go after the law. The law came after the people and harassed them any way they could. Let's just say the park ranger got a little history lesson out on the water that night.

CHAPTER THIRTY-TWO

Stealing Back the Job

It was a stormy January night, and it was raining like hell. They had a tropical storm coming in. On the boat, the wind was blowing about thirty-five miles an hour. And it was rough as hell. This was a job that was already planned and scheduled to be there that night.

Leaving the dock in the storm, it was a dark dreary night, with lightning. No one wanted to go, but they had to get the job in. Miserable to say the least. They had to load twenty-five thousand pounds into smaller boats in that bad weather, and they were setting at Joes Camp Key. After an hour of sitting and waiting to make contact with the boat, it finally happened. The boat was a larger shrimp boat, so the guys had to run to the boat because it could not get that close to shore. It was brought into Pavillion and Little Pavillion Key, trying to stay on the leeward side and trying to stay out of the wind. Offloading the boat, getting one boat and another and another, after about two hours, we got everything unloaded and sent the smaller boats on their way. They headed in, and the shrimp boat headed a little offshore to hold against the weather. The smaller boats were getting beat all to hell out there. On the way into Chokoloskee, visibility was low, so they ran a little slow to make sure everything was okay in front of them. They brought the load onto Choloskee island and got rid of it. The vans were sitting there, waiting. The crew commented that this one was one of the easiest jobs they had ever done. Because of the weather, they didn't have to worry about the law interfering in any way. Money was delivered in the next couple of days, and it was great.

As the next few days continued, the Daniels crew got a message that they had to do another job, and the message came into them as soon as they offloaded the thirty thousand pounds they had to take an ex-navy vessel and sink it in an area about eighty feet deep. To keep this next boat and go offshore and sink an eighty-foot metal hull boat. They were told it was an ex-old navy vessel.

Kent said, "The navy vessel?"

And they responded, "Yes. When you guys get through, you are going to take everyone off the boat but two people, and then you are going to take it offshore and sank it. Whenever they sink the boat, the last two people will bring the crab boat in." They did not want to get caught with it in their possession.

They were all sitting around at Plover Key, and the crab boat was on its way. Sitting around talking on the T-Craft, someone said how much was on this one, and Kent responded thirty thousand pounds. Somebody said, "Thirty thousand? That must be a big boat."

Kent responded, "Yes, it is. It is an almost eighty-foot long metal hull boat."

"After they finished offloading the boat, bring the crew guys back with you., and we are taking everyone off the boat but two people because it is going offshore to be sunk."

They offloaded, and whenever it was offloaded, it was taken to deeper water offshore in eighty feet of water and sunk it. They got the radio call, and they got the boat as close to Plover Key so they can run out and meet them, off-loading. With the boats offloaded, half the boats went on the east side of the island, and the other half was going to the west side of the island, so it was being offloaded in two different places. Both were to be put in the garages of two different houses, and they were to wait till the next day to send it out. Kent took his group to the east side of the island and unloaded their cargo in the garage of the house. Everything went off without a hitch.

After completion of this job, the guys had to hurry because they had another job to do that night. They had to get this one in quick, and they were pushing for time, and they would turn the boat around and send it right back out to the new job waiting.

Heading back out, they eased across the bay and headed to where the other boat was supposed to be waiting. They got there and started to offload on to the boat, then they had to sit there and wait for the instructions on where this load was going. After the third boat showed, Kent saw Darryl and asked. "Where is this job going?"

Darryl replied, "Odolph's."

On the way in, Randal saw a boat sitting in Cholokoloskee Bay right in Rutter Bar Pass, thinking it was one of the boats that may have broken down. Realizing it was a park ranger, Randal showered down on the motor giving it to full throttle, and the chase was on. Randal came on the radio and said, "I have sharks behind me. I have sharks behind me."

Kent looked up and saw the blue lights, and he told the crew, "We can cut them off."

Kent told the crew that he only needed one guy, not both, so Audie said, "I will go." When they got alongside the ranger doing sixty and Randal doing the forty miles an hour, and spotlighted the ranger so they could blind him so the ranger could not tell which way the Randal left. They knew they only had about ten to fifteen minutes before the other Rangers got there, and they held him there for several minutes until Randal got away. Kent came on the radio and told the other boats that he got this, and he kept the light on the ranger so he could not move so the ranger backed off. Kent went in front of the ranger and kept the light on him so he could not see which way the boat went. After the other boats arrived and they headed in, they offloaded, and another job completed by the Daniels clan, and another one well done.

Two different crews had jobs that night, and the crews didn't get together. It was hard to get to talk to each other. This was another two-job night.

The weather was calm at the moment but was about change and break down on them at any time. It was 6:00 PM when a big boat was coming in to be offloaded. A call was made to the local authorities, and the marine patrol (FWC) and the coast guard were informed that the mother boat was followed into shore. Upon arriving at Pavillion, they anchored it off due to the fact that they had seen the coast guard following them. The crew that was meeting the boat came on out and removed all of the crew members from the boat and hauled ass, leaving everything on board to sit there. The crew from the other organization sat back and watched the marine patrol and the park rangers board the boat. The next morning, the other organization would watch the authorities go on and off the boat for hours at a time. Now the other organization placed a crab boat not really close but close enough to watch what the authorities with what they were doing with the boat. After that, they realized that there was a gap in time with the shift change of the authorities when the boat would be left unattended. This was the opportunity the other organization needed to bring in the closer. The closer was notorious for finishing up the jobs no one else could get done within their organization.

So they called in Tommy, one of the bigger and larger-than-life men who was not afraid of trying anything. Tommy called the Daniels crew because he needs the best of the best to organize the offloading and bring the job in. With a different organization at the helm of the job, they were calling all shots and making the decisions. It was agreed upon by the Daniels crew and Tommy that they would wait for the authorities to leave the boat, and Tommy was going to drop off a crab boat onto the large boat. Before Tommy boarded the boat, Tommy paid the park rangers five thousand dollars for one hour of time on the boat. Before Tommy boarded the boat, it was understood with the captain of the crab boat that once Tommy moved the boat, they were to move into his spot and let the authorities board them and check them out. It was also understood that they were to pretend that they were having engine problems and they were just working on getting it repaired.

When Tommy boarded the boat, he checked it from end to end, making sure he was the only one on board. After completing his check, he then proceeded to pull the anchor and fired up the engine. Once he was ready, he engaged the thrust and took off. He drove the boat five miles and hid the boat behind an island on the backside of

Plover Key so that it would not be picked up on radar. Once the boat was sitting behind the island, the Daniels crew moved into action. When they hit Plover Key, it was game on. The Daniels crew got that boat unloaded in record time. Tommy and the Daniels crew had arranged for four different T-craft boats to be sitting inshore of Lumbar Key in four different areas so they could run interference for the marijuana to be hauled in they needed. If all else failed, they even were ready to ram a boat if they need be. All four boats were used as decoys.

The boats were now loaded, and they were heading to Chattam. They were going to put part of the bales into house hammock and the other half in a whiskey still creek, all except for one boatload that was carrying three thousand pounds, which would be held for payment for the Daniels crew doing their job. Once everything was in the creek, the crab boat had been called. The crab boat let them know that they were coming in from the Florida Keys when the boat started running hot. After the marine patrol searched all night, they finally found the boat in Flubber, but when they boarded her, they found no drugs or anyone on the boat. So this was the night that the marijuana smugglers stole the load back away from the authorities and got away it.

The captain asked the marine patrol, "What in the hell are you looking for?"

The marine patrol said, "for drugs," as they went over the boat with a fine-tooth comb.

Two boats would go out just before dark. One would go north, and one would go south on the outside. Then in thirty more minutes, two more boats would leave, and they continued this until they had six boats out. Three thousand pounds were put on each boat. Then the watch guy would go back with them. They left two people out in the mangroves watching the loads that were stashed. And they would be there until the stuff was moved. Since this was a Totch job, the first load of twelve thousand out of Whiskey Creek was nice and easy, with the watch boats ahead and behind it, and it went into the ranger station in Everglades City. The following night the rest of the bales were moved to different locations to be moved out of the area.

They were taken to Houston to cross over to Turners River to Halfway Creek to Plantation Island. Everything was loaded onto box trucks and vans and taken to the homestead to their local drop-off point and waiting to be paid.

Since the authorities lost this job and were figuring that the Daniels crew was the one who had done it, they started to bug the phones, and they were getting family members out of jail and having them embedded into their organization so they would become a snitch. They offered time served for doing this, and it was very tempting for someone who was going to be in jail for a very long time. The immediate family was not close to Leon, but the family did get a phone call warning about Leon being placed with them. When the message was told to Randal, the family had a meeting, and the family was told about the warning. Randal would not hire him, but the captains were allowed to pick their own crew; obviously this man was picked to be on one of the boats to be a crew member.

CHAPTER THIRTY-THREE

The Rock Pit

As spring arrived Kent was told he was heading to Columbia. Kent received a call from the Daniels crew and was asked if he was at home because they needed to come by the house and speak to him about doing another run. After their meeting, he was picking up the phone and letting Johnny know they had another fishing trip and what they were going to need as far as food, fuel, and supplies and to be sure they had enough beer and alcohol for a six-day trip. Johnny got everything ready, had the boat taken down from her cradle, and was launched and being prepared to go. Kent telling Johnny they were going to leave the dock the next morning before daybreak, and Kent had instructed him to pick him up at the airport. Another organization that the Daniels clan worked for had informed him that they added a new addition to their team; he was a radar radio operator for the United States coast guard. Kent figured this would be an easy job, so he figured he would captain the boat and would not have to hire someone else to do it, and it would be an easy ride.

Necocli, Colombia, was the destination for the job. Fifteen thousand pounds of marijuana would be loaded and transported on the *Bluebird*. Kent thought this destination was a little strange but agreed because it would save him a little time.

Kent flew to Marathon, got a room at the Sea Horse Motel, and the next morning, Johnny picked him up at three-thirty in the morning. When Kent got in the truck with Johnny, he went over all of the instructions he was given and what was going to take place. Kent then went over all of the fuel requirements and how much freshwater would need to be put on the boat. Johnny looked at Kent and told him he had enough supplies for eight days. Kent said that was perfect because "we do not have to go that far to get this one, Johnny," then asked how much they were going to be putting on the boat, and Kent replied fifteen thousand.

Johnny then responded, "That's a light one for the *Bluebird*." Johnny, laughing, said, "Damn, did you tell them we would be back in six nights?"

And Kent responded, "You are not going to believe this." He then told him about the new coast guard radar radio operator in their pocket, and he was going to lead them home.

"Damn then, it should be an easy ride."

Going over to Colombia, the water was nice and beautiful, with a three-foot sea and light wind. When the weather was good like this, there was nothing better than being on the open water. Going straight across to the pickup destination, they came across birds flying across the water and fishing from the sea, and then seeing dozens of dolphin pods that played in the wake of the boat that they watched on their way through. Upon arrival and tying the boat up to the dock a being greeted by the locals, they asked how long they were going to be with them. Kent responded, "Just overnight." Kent explained that he was meeting a friend, and the guy started laughing. Kent said, "Damn, you must be the friend."

The man responded, "Yes, I am."

He then told Kent they were going to get him to move the boat down a little and then asked, "Where would you like us to put the bales, on top or under the deck?"

Kent replied, "Under, so we don't have to worry too much going home."

That evening, they loaded the *Bluebird*, and they were ready to leave, but they were waiting on the guy that they usually sent back with them who was called the watcher. Once he showed up, and they checked the engines for oil and water, they left and headed out at four o'clock that morning.

Getting closer to Cuba that evening, Kent noticed around the Dry Tortugas area that there was a lot of boat traffic on the radar. Kent told Johnny, "I guess we are going to see if this guy is worth the money that they paid him, if not, we are going to be busted." An hour later, the two-way radio went off calling the *Bluebird*, so Kent reached up and answered the call and was informed that he better start looking for another route to come in on because the coast guard was sitting right in their path. He advised them to either sit and wait or find another route. Kent then told the radio operator he would be there as planned, meaning he would find another route.

Kent started talking to Johnny. "Let's go up the straights and go between Cuba and Hatti and bring the load on in." Johnny agreed, and they came through that night at one o'clock in the morning, and this put Kent one hundred miles out of his way. When he came through that area, he turned and was going to head toward lower Matacumbee Bridge, and since he had a net on the back of the boat, he would look like any other mackerel fisherman coming from the Miami area.

After about halfway there to Matacumbee, easing along, they received another radio call letting Kent know there was a change of plans and asked for his location, Kent told him, and the radio operator said to hold until a message could be delivered to him. As always, an airplane flew overhead a couple of hours later and dropped a bottle out of the window with a note in it. The note was in a bottle that would be dropped as close to the boat as possible, and the lid would be taped down so it was airtight. They had gaff poles on the boat to catch the end bowie, and they would use them to fish the bottle out of the water. The note said Everglades was hot, another bust happened there, and it gave him a new location that he needed to be at by eleven o'clock that evening.

Kent turned and headed toward the Seven Mile Bridge. Coming under the Seven Mile Bridge an hour just before dark crossing over from the Atlantic Ocean to the Gulf of Mexico side, they were sitting there, and Kent explained to the crew that they got there a little too early. Kent told the crew they could go out there and start looking for fish if they wanted to, or if they had any suggestions, he was all ears.

Johnny said, "I would like to have a hot meal and a drink."

Kent explained, "You are going to be having that soon enough, aren't you. By tomorrow, you will be at your house." Johnny had this stupid grin on his face, and Kent knew something was up. Kent replied, "What in the hell do you have on your mind, Johnny?"

"Let's take the boat into Fara Banco and have a hot meal and a drink."

Kent looked at him and said, "With this shit on board?"

Johnny said, "Yes, we will just tie up to the dock and go eat and keep an eye on the boat while we are there."

Kent replied, "What happens if someone gets on the boat?"

Johnny said, "We aren't going to be there but a couple of hours." And the other crew had agreed to stay on the boat when they were in the bar eating. Since they were outnumbered, and everyone had a say, they proceeded to the dock at Fara Blanco.

They eased their way in and tied up, went upstairs, and ordered a couple of drinks and some food; not many people were there. They sat there and got themselves something to eat, and Kent told Johnny to take some food to the other crew member that was left on the boat, and he would pay the tab, and they could be on their way. They pulled away from the dock and eased back into the Gulf of Mexico. They arrived at the location, which was a rock pit or quarry, and they pulled up and they told Kent to bring her up and run the boat aground so they could offload her.

The crew had already removed the bales from below the deck to the top and had it waiting to be offloaded. They brought down two front-end loader with two men in the bucket, and they jumped on the boat, and they started throwing the bales in the bucket as quickly as they could, and the front-end loader would go up on dry land and drop it off, and they would continue to do this until it was completely unloaded. Once they were unloaded, they pushed them back in the water, and they went offshore and cleaned the boat out, making sure nothing was left in the boat, like they always did, and then they headed back to the dock and tied her up.

Kent went to the motel. Kent picked up the phone and called home to let everyone know everything was good, then asked what had gone on in Everglades City, he heard it was hot. Daddy was telling Kent that a crab boat got busted, and when they tried to run from the coast guard, they shot across the bow of the boat and then let them know that the next one they would sink them. Since Operation Everglades had happened, the coast guard had been given new power and making them a little more aggressive toward the smugglers. The captain of the boat stopped the boat and boarded them with guns drawn on the crew and the captain. They were told to go to the back of the boat and lie face down on the deck and were handcuffed and held on the deck of the boat for four hours. They were not even allowed to go use the bathroom; if they had to go, it was in their pants. The coast guard didn't care, and they were showing their force.

The next morning, Kent wanted to fly home, but his dad told him to wait there. They were going to fly down and see him. Kent then told Johnny to get her fueled back up and wait for the next set of instructions. The job they just finished was great, with no problems in the job to be added to their portfolio.

Randal landed in Marathon and went to talk to Kent. He explained that there was another job out in the center of the Gulf of Mexico, almost 120 miles off of Dry Tortuga. Leaving the dock around ten o'clock in the morning, Johnny had the boat fueled, and all supplies were loaded and ready to go.

Kent was going to run down the gulf side, so he was hidden by the island. Getting closer to the boat, Kent was still trying to make radio contact with the other boat that was broken down, and it never answered Kent. Kent felt a little cautious when this happened. Thinking that the batteries were dead on the boat, because they told him that the alternators went out on it. Slowing the boat down and bringing up the hydrofoils two miles away from the boat, Kent looked at Johnny and said, "The boat doesn't look right, it looks like there is another boat tied on the other side of the boat behind it." He then looked through the binoculars and could see there was another coast guard boat hiding on the other side of it, and it looked like that boat had already been busted. Looking at Johnny he said, "If I turn and run, they are going to chase us."

And Johnny replied, "They are sending a zodiac with two agents on board out over to the *Bluebird*."

They contacted the bluebird and told them to communicate with them on channel sixteen. They told them not to move and stay right where they were. Kent looked at Johnny and said, "We have to get this two-way radio off the mount and hide it and make it look like it is not being used." Taking it off the mount, they hid it under one of the bunks and hid the radio in a compartment under the mattress.

The coast guard came up and asked Kent if they could board the boat, and Kent said, "Yes, come on aboard." They asked what his business was that he was doing in that area. Kent replied, "We were looking for fish," since they had a net on the boat. He really didn't care what the coast guard said.

The coast guard replied, "You are hunting fish in this deep of water."

Kent tried to explain that the fish came from offshore and would head to shallow water." He said when he saw the boat, he slowed down and didn't want to look suspicious.

The agent responded, "Sir, it looked like you were running straight at this bat."

Kent then said, "Sir, we fish this area all the time."

He looked at Kent and said, "You have no problem searching the boat."

Kent said, "No, I have no problem, we are a fishing vessel."

The agent went through the engine room and every compartment he could find on that boat.

Looking at Kent and the crew, he asked for their IDs.

They handed him their driver's license.

Looking at Kent's license, he started laughing a little bit and said, "So you are from Everglades City."

Kent looked back at the agent and said, "Yes, I am, so what?"

He said, "Do you know what happened off the coast of Everglades yesterday?"

Kent replied, "No, I do not, I have been out here fishing for the last four nights."

The guy finally finished searching the boat and told the head agent that the boat was clean.

Looking around the wheelhouse, he found a piece of paper that he damn sure did not need to find.

The paper that was dropped to him out of the airplane from a gallon jug from two jobs ago.

The agent looked at Kent and said, "We have heard a lot about this boat, the *Bluebird*."

Kent asked him what he was implying.

"I am not implying anything, and I am just going to let you know this boat will be watched. We will know everything about this boat, where she is docked, and when she is moved, everything."

Kent looked at him and said, "Are we free to go?"

Getting back on their boat, he looked at Kent and pointed his finger at him and said, "Mr. Daniels, I will catch you later."

At that point, Kent, being the smartass he was, said that he could catch him at the local bar in about six hours and that Kent would buy the first round.

Every time the boat would leave the dock after that, they would be tailed or stopped by the coast guard.

Kent knew the bluebird had done the last job.

He didn't want the coast guard getting their hands on this boat because he felt like there was a local boat builder out of Key West that could get in trouble for the hydrofoils that were put on the boat.

Kent then went to Billy Tyner and asked him to strip the boat and he could have everything he took off.

Billy asked, "Why, Kent? This is a good boat."

Kent explained the boat was hot as hell, and it needed to be gone.

After a few days, Billy had the engines removed and sold for Kent, and then Kent and Billy took the boat offshore in six hundred feet of water and sunk her. The *Bluebird* was lost and gone forever and had done its last job.

Like most organizations, you had to stop and think that family was not always blood. This business was a brotherhood of trust, and they were like a family. The guys that Kent had on the boat were not just friends; it was a brotherhood, and they took care of each other. Kent always included the crew about where they went as much as Kent himself. There was one thing about these people; they trusted each other with their life. Kent trusted them to take care of him, and the crew knew and trusted that Kent would not let anything happen to them. This was a mutual respect that they had for each other, and it was never deviated from.

CHAPTER THIRTY-FOUR

Unexpected Visit

In early summer an unexpected visit came to Florida from a friend Kent met in Columbia. A guy Kent would do business with when he would take the bluebird across the water. When Kent was down there, he befriended this man, and he would tell him about all of the wildlife adventures and the hunting that was done off an airboat. Kent being the person that he was, he told the gentlemen that if he ever made it to America to look him up, and he would take him out hunting for a deer or a hog and even frogging off the airboat so he could see what the Everglades was all about. This gentleman was one the guys who was in charge of the growing farm, and he owned a plantation that he cultivated Columbian Gold, and he was the main supplier that Kent had dealt with. Kent believed that this guy that was named Hector was Estavan's right-hand man.

Because Kent was one of the captains that would haul his product back into the United States, they became close friends, and they trusted each other. When Kent was there, they would go out drinking, and Hector would bring Kent to his home to eat dinner and continue drinking, and they both had a lot of respect for each other. This guy had heard about the fight Kent had with the monkey that had gone abroad and whipped Kent on the boat. He told Kent that he heard how fond he was of the monkey and, he wanted to make sure Kent would have one to take back with him as a gift.

Kent replied, "No, no, no. There are no monkeys allowed on my boat."

Laughing, Hector replied, "I understand, *cabeza dura.*"

When Kent would go to Colombia, this man would take Kent through the fields and show him how they grew and cultivated it and packaged the product to be sent to the United States. When some of the plants would bud, the plant itself would grow to six to eight feet tall. The strength of the pot came from the bud and how it was grown. This man had some of the best Columbian Gold you could ask for, and when Kent was there, he asked him to try some of his red hair or redbud, which was more potent than the Columbian Gold.

The phone rang one night, and Lucinda, Kent's girlfriend at the time, came to Kent and said there was a Spanish-speaking guy on the phone and he was asking to speak to "you, El Capitan."

Hector told Kent, "I am here."

Kent replied, "Where are you?"

Hector said, "Miami."

Kent replied, "Where are you?"

Hector told Kent, "I am at the hotel at the airport."

Kent responded, "I will be there in a couple of hours."

Hector replied, "I have a gift for you, El Capitan."

Kent started laughing. "As long as it is no monkey, right."

Hector said, "No monkey."

Kent left in his Bronco and headed to the hotel at the airport in Miami. Upon arrival, Kent found his room and knocked on the door. When he opened the door, he hugged Kent and told him to let him get his gift in the bedroom. Kent looked wary and said, "Hector, I said no monkey."

Hector started laughing and said, "I have something better than a monkey." This was a new strain of marijuana that Hector had just started growing. Kent opened it up and started looking at it and started smelling it. When Kent saw it, it looked as though it had red hair in it, and Hector told Kent this is a new strain. "I think we can get more for it than the other I am growing. This is a gift for you, please take it and show it around to your people and see if we can do anything with it."

Kent and Hector got in the Bronco and started back to the Everglades. He told Hector that he would take him out on the airboat in the morning and see if they could kill a deer or hog. When they arrived, they went to the local tavern and had a few drinks and dinner then headed back to the house for the night.

The next day, they got up and packed up and cooked some fresh fish, and then around one o'clock that afternoon, they hooked up the airboat. They took some stuff down to the camp, and on the way down they came across a bear that was spooked by the airboat's noise. Sitting around, they built a campfire and had a few drinks, and then Kent told Hector that he had to get a few things ready on the boat because they were getting ready to go hunting.

Getting back on the airboat running across the marshlands at a high rate of speed and with Hector sitting ready with a gun in hand, they came across a hog running out of a thick wooded area. They chased the hog and shot and killed him. They put the hog on the bow of the boat, and they headed out to see if they could have found the deer. Just about sundown at dusk, they came across a big buck that was ahead of them, about a quarter of a mile, when the laid chase; he started running for a head of land to try to get away from the airboat and noise.

Now heading back to the camp to dress the animals that they had hunted, and upon arrival, they had dressed them out, when Kent took a piece of each one to cook for that's night dinner.

Asking Hector after he had eaten, "What do you think?"

Hector responded, "Pretty well, I like it."

Then Kent asked, "Are you ready for a drink?"

After the drinks and sitting around the fire and talking and having good time, Kent looked at Hector and said, "The moon is almost down."

"Are you ready to go gigging for frogs?"

Hector said, "Sure."

So they climbed on the airboat and left to start their journey of hunting for the frogs. Once Kent came across the frogs, Kent showed Hector how to gig them, and he took a few tries before he got the hang of it. Around one o'clock in the morning, they returned back to the camp; they went inside and lay down. Kent got up early the next morning and left Hector sleeping, and Kent cleaned the frogs and was cooking them up when Hector smelled the food cooking and coffee brewing. Hector then told Kent that he needed to wash up a little bit to get ready for breakfast. When Hector came back, they sat down and ate breakfast, and they then proceeded to clean everything, uploaded the boat, and heading back through the Everglades heading in. On the trip to the house, Kent decided to teach Hector how to drive the airboat. Hector enjoyed himself and loved running the boat.

As the guys returned to the house, they loaded Hector's stuff in the bronco so Kent could take him back to Miami, and he thanked him for the gift and promised that they would see each other real soon.

CHAPTER THIRTY-FIVE

Praying for a Safe Return

It was a dark, rainy, and gloomy night before they left the dock. The crew and Randal had a real heart to heart with them about the job they were about to do. This was a night when the law was all over the place, but they had a boat that needed to come in and offload, so if there was anyone who did not want to go, please say it now because this one was going to be tough one, and out of all the jobs that they had done, this was the one that had the highest chance of being busted, and they could all end up in jail.

The crew responded out of ten boats, ten said yes, they are going, and this was what they did. The boats were going to run light because with that many boats, they could divide the marijuana and thus give less weight per boat. Which made the boat run a lot lighter, especially in rough weather. The weight was just enough to keep the boat from being pounded in the waves.

Easing away from the dock, realizing that no jobs ever left from Mamas and Daddy's house, Kent looked back and could see Mama standing on the porch and looking out over the water and praying. She had said she was worried about this job, and she had a knot in her stomach about it and was sure she was not going to relax until everyone made it home safe.

Meeting up at Pavilion, all the boats gathered closer to the beach on the south end of the island so they would not be detected and out of sight anyone coming by at a distance. Sitting there for thirty to forty minutes, the crew was running high with anxiety, waiting to see if that boat had been busted.

The radio came on, and they heard another crew's boat calling. "The coast guard is closing in on me because I can see him on radar." He was running with no lights on, and then coming in from another direction was the boat they were waiting on. They recognized the voice on the radio as a local boy from Everglades by the name of Captain David that had gone offshore to pick up another load with another crew. One of their guys had let the cat out of the bag about their job coming through Jewel Key, which was about four miles from where they were.

The crew was sitting there, and that was Captain David, and they were about to get them. Maybe they stood a chance, but the coast guard was closing in on him.

Randal was listening to the other captain, and he turned to the crew and said, "Boys, I can't let the other crew get busted, so I am going to get the crew off that boat. They have family, and there is no reason for them to go down with the job." Randal then instructed the other crew on his boat to call the boat they were waiting on, knowing they were going to meet the boat offshore. Randal told the other crew member he would be late, but he would be there. He instructed the crew when they contacted the other boat to tell him to turn his light on and off really fast so they could see where he was, and the captain came back and said he has a dim flashlight that he would turn towards the bow of the boat so it could not be seen on the radar.

The captain came on the two-way radio that had special chips in it that no one else could hear but them. "I have the other boat on radar, and they are five miles behind him, but they have another boat behind them running fast from inshore."

The answer on the radio was "We know." The boat was asked to turn his light on and off fast.

The boat came on and said, "You are heading right to me, and I am going to stop right here. I have you on the radar." In about two to three minutes they were tied alongside the big boat and unloading it as quickly as they could with all of the bales already sitting on the deck.

Just about the time they had started loading the boats, the captain came back to the guys and said, "We have another boat coming straight at them."

The guys said, "Is it only one boat?"

And the captain replied, "Yes."

And they said, "It's okay, that would be Randal."

Randal got everything loaded, and Randal asked, "What do you want to do? Do you want to come with us or what?"

The captain responded. "I don't have anything on this boat, what can they do. We washed her down already."

Randal replied, "Okay then, you handle it."

The crew stayed on the big boat with the captain. And Randal and his crew were leaving, and they agreed to go to the gator hole next to the auger hole., Then he asked, "Everyone knows where this is, right?"

"Yes," everyone responded.

And he then told them to make sure they all came into the area from different directions. This area was in the mangroves, so it would be a great place to stash the bales. As they started to leave, the blue lights came on in the distance, and they could see the other boat was being busted, with the coast guard right behind them. Randal knew the shit was getting ready to come down, and they knew the ranger, the marine patrol, and even the Federal guys would be there with their helicopter in tow. They were offshore ten miles, so they knew they had to do something quickly.

When the lights came on, the crew all told each other, "We will see you at home," and they all took off in a different direction, and they knew it was every man for themselves.

They left the big boat running as fast as they could to get to Pavillion because they need the cover of that island so that radar could not pick them up. There were a thousand things going through Kent's mind at that time, trying to make sure everyone arrived safely. Finally, they made it to Pavillion, and they were sitting behind it.

Kent slowed the boat down and told the crew, "Let's have a drink to calm our nerves down a little."

One of the crew guys lit a cigarette, and Kent told him to smoke it while he could because that cigarette could be seen for miles away. The boats were ahead of Kent about a mile or so. So they got the boat back on top and started running again to the gator hole.

Off in a distance back toward Marco Island, Kent saw this damn light in the air coming up, and Kent tapped the crew on the shoulder and pointed at the light, and the crew said, "What in the hell are we going to do?"

Kent replied, "I don't know, but whatever it is, we need to do it now." Looking back towards Rabbit Key, Kent saw the blue lights coming out, and he hoped that the blue light was heading to the crab boat that they had offloaded Looking at his crew, Kent said, "We have a change of plans, and we are going to Charlie Creek, and we can put the stuff up there fast because I want to get away from them as fast as we can."

Easing his way down Charlie's Creek, the waterway was getting tighter and tighter. They finally found a good place to put the stuff with a good cover of foliage. They put a brown tarp down, got everything unloaded on to the tarp, and placed a green tarp as cover for it so no one could see it out of a helicopter or airplane.

Coming out of the creek, Kent shut the motor off, and it sounded clear. Kent looked at the crew and said, "I need to make sure no one comes in this creek in a couple of days." So if you look under the console of the boat, they tied from one mangrove root to another with a fishing string across Joe's Creek. He looked at his crew and said, "Guys, I am heading home." They asked if they were going to check on the other crew and Kent replied no. He said he would call them on the radio. He then keyed the mike and said, "I am good, my net is on the boat, and everything looks good, and I am heading home."

They came on and replied to Kent, "We have almost got our net on the boat, and everything is looking good."

Kent got to the dock and tied up the boat and sent the crew on home, and he sat on the porch and talked to his mom and told her everything was all right.

Randal came up and asked, "What happened to you?"

Kent replied, "I put mine in Charlies Creek and put up a line to make sure no one gets in the creek."

Randal then asked Kent, "I need you to do me a favor."

Kent said, "What?"

Randal replied, "I need you to run the crew to Everglades for me."

Kent said, "No problem, I am going that way anyway."

They climbed in the Bronco and headed to Everglades City.

On the way to Everglades, "That was a brave thing that your dad had done for us to get us off the boat," David said. "I wasn't sure if it was him or the law." Then David said Randal told him there was no sense in not getting paid. He looked over and saw the bales on the deck and told the crew to grab ten and let's go. "At least you will get paid."

Getting to Everglades City to the circle, all hell broke loose. The cops came out from everywhere. They snatched them out of the car, and they asked them, "Where in the hell have you been."

Kent replied that some asshole kept throwing the blue lights on and scared the fish, but the boys were dressed in their Sunday go-to meeting white fishing boots that the town always joked about. So they held them there for an hour and a half, and then Kent told them, "If you have anything on us, arrest us, but if you don't have anything on us or if you just want to screw with us, then you better let us go." He told the crew, "Get in, and I will take you home, they have no business holding us." So they got in and left. Kent took them home, and then he went home and went to bed.

The next day, getting up and sitting around talking to Daddy, Kent asked, "When do you think we are going to be able to go get the job."

Randal responded, "I have no idea, it is still hot around here."

Kent told his dad that they held him on the side of the road last night. Randal asked them, "What did you tell them?"

Kent said, "I told them we were fishing, but some asshole ran the fish off." And then Kent told them to arrest him or let him go.

Sitting there at the table, Kent looked at his dad and said, "We need to start getting it in, but it's hot. I think if I can get two men and one boat and go get the stuff that he hid in the creek."

Randal responded, "I'll take a couple of boats and run in the opposite way to keep the heat off of you. When I get to the creek and if the string is still there, I will go on in and get it."

Kent explained, "Give me thirty minutes, and that way the heat will be on y'all." Kent said, "Where do you want to bring it to?"

Randal said, "We will have a van here, bring her to the dock, and I'll have a driver here to move it."

That evening, Kent and the crew left and got outside of Turners River, and they got outside of Pavillion and shut the engine off and had a drink and a cigarette. He told the crew to keep a lookout and ran over to Joes Key and, they cut the engine. Again, no sound was there, and the string was still intact, and the crew said, "Which way are we going home?"

Kent said, "Secret Creek to Rutter Bar, and stay close to the islands." And they went home with no problems. They got to the dock and unloaded everything in the van, and they started her up.

Kent got on the radio and said, "My net is on the boat and everything is good."

The guys came back and told him, "There are sharks in my net tonight." But Kent knew that they had nothing on the boat, so they were good. The next morning, the driver came for the van and rolled her right out of town.

Just before evening, Kent had left the house and went to the store to get some soda and some other stuff he was going to need on the boat. As he was putting the stuff in the back of the Bronco, a park ranger came over and told Kent that "If you guys were going to do anything, the first four hours are going to be clear tonight with no one on the water because everyone is going to be in a meeting, so if you are going to do anything, this would be the time, because after that, it is going to come alive."

Kent went back to his dad's and told his dad what the rangers just told them. Randal responded that the sheriffs said that they knew the stuff was in the gator hole, so if they were going to move it, this was when they needed to do it.

One of the northern fishermen that frequented their area saw the limbs busted, and he told the ranger He saw what was hidden, and he told them where it was.

Kent told them, "I am fueled up and ready to go."

"I don't want to run everybody at the same time, take two boats at a time, and go the way you did last night. I am going to wait for thirty minutes and start out. Keep your radio on you, and when you get loaded and run to John Daniels Cove, and at ten o'clock, I want you to ease across the bay and take it to the old abandoned fish house."

Kent asked, "Are we going to put it in the truck?"

Randal responded, "No, we are going to put it in the freezer."

At ten, Kent eased across and got to the old fish house and loaded everything in the old freezer and locked the door, and he took off across the bay, and they sat there until they got a radio call. The radio came on and said, "My net is on the boat, and we are at the dock, and everything is good."

They asked Kent what he was going to do, and he told them, "At twelve o'clock, it is going to come alive out here, so I am going another way, and we won't all be going across in the same direction at the same time."

When Kent hit Lopez River heading through, he was going over to cross the creek to duck head; he ran across two boats sitting still. Kent looked at the crew and said, "Boys, hang on, this is going to be a fun time. Kent opened up both motors wide open and knew that if he went back offshore, he would be endangering the boats. He headed to Turners River heading to Chokoloskee and hid behind the oyster bar and cut the engines, and they could hear the boats coming, but when you had wind, the foam trail off the back of the boat disappeared pretty fast so, Kent and the crew were watching them.

Kent said, "Something doesn't look right. How many boats did you see? I only saw one that's right, but there were two."

So they sat there for twenty minutes longer. They sat there and had another drink, and as sure as the stars were shining that night, here came the other boat. Kent was waiting for them to get on the other side of the bay, and he eased his boat across the other side, and he was heading to the dock when the neighbor said to tie the boat up here because they were waiting for him at the other end.

"Tie it to my dock." And right across the canal was Mom and Dad's place. So they got up there to his house and sat there for a little bit. Kent asked if he could use this phone.

Kent said, "I am right across the canal from you."

Randal responded, "I saw you come in."

An hour or so later, the guy took them to Dad's house.

CHAPTER THIRTY-SIX

Whisper Jets

It was March, and the winds were known to blow hard in this month, and there was no exception. The wind was blowing twenty-five to thirty miles an hour out of the southwest. The seas were four to six feet in height. A boat should never leave the dock in this type of weather because the seas were too rough, but the clan had no choice because the boat was coming, and they could not control the weather.

They were heading to Little Pavillion Key sitting behind the island, blocking the waves, and waiting on the radio call and the all-too-familiar sound of the exhaust bubbling in the water of the large boat coming in.

The clan had another job coming in as well because they were now the only crew in this area. The other crews were busted, and the Daniels group was picking up the slack of the other crews that were no longer there.

Most of the jobs that they had done that were double were sixty thousand, and these tonight were eighty thousand. They had nine T-crafts that were meeting the larger boats, and this way, they could keep the boats lighter so the seas would not roll over the boat and sink the boat.

The radio call came in on the two boats, and they met them on the back of Little Pavillion to block the seas as much as they could. They started off-loading after getting everything loaded in the small t-craft, and at this time, the government came out with the whisper jet, which was very quiet. It was a low hissing sound coming straight to them from the distance ahead. Half of the boats went one way, and the other boats went another to keep them moving in different directions.

The captain came out of the cabin and yelled at the crew, "We have boats coming to us."

And they asked, "How far are they out?"

And the captain returned by saying, "About four miles out."

They now realized the whispering sound was the jets circling above them. They knew at this point the coast guard and marine patrol were coming up all around them. The larger vessels were the coast guard, and the ones coming from shore were the park rangers and the marine patrol.

The captain then yelled, "Every boat for itself."

"Put it anywhere." they yelled. "Just get it off your boats."

Everybody ran in all different directions, and Kent ran further offshore of Pavillion, running hard and fast and, he told the crew to hang onto whatever they could because at this point, there was no turning back.

Randal opened the boats engine up to go as fast as it could go. As they approach Rabbit Key, one of his crewmen asked to slow the boat down he wanted off. The crewman dove overboard and swam to the nearby island.

Randal told him, "What the hell, you are crazy," so Randal slowed, and he dove overboard.

The reason he dove off the boat was Randal thought the crewman was trying to get away from the law, but he could not understand that because Randal knew the water better than the crewman did. This was the area that the Daniels clan knew the Green doors, and there were a lot of them. A green door was a spot that they could go through the mangroves and they would open up into other creeks, allowing them to get away.

Kent, now running deeper out to sea, was still running hard and fast, just trying to stay one step in front of the law, and Kent figured if he could just stay far enough ahead of them, they would not chase him. Kent was hitting the waves hard and fast when the boat started jumping the waves, and when the boat hit the water, the boat would shake and vibrate so hard, it would rattle your knees. It would jar your knees so hard he could barely stay standing. Running with five thousand pounds on the boat and with the weather and the rough seas, it took a big toll on the boat he was running in. Several helicopters with spotlights were up and on. The whisper jet was in the air. There were so many lights on that it looked like they were in a big city with all the lights on it.

Kent, running as hard as he could to the Houston River to get to the Shell Islands to get to Sunday Bay. Houston River was a hard river to maneuver in because of the lower tide and the oyster bars. Knowing if there was a bit behind him losing them or running them aground. He got through Houston River into Houston Bay and now was on his way into Sunday Bay. Kent was looking for a new river, which was a tight narrow creek, and looking for the green door that would lead them into the mangroves, which was a real thick plant that had branches that would bounce back, and you would never know they were there and would open up into another creek that was just wide enough for the boat.

Now Kent was through the green door, and he was looking for a good place to put the bales so they could not be seen from the air or they had to stay at dry end up out of the water. They unloaded the boat and stashed the bales, and the crew would break limbs and cover the bales and cover and hide the stash. They sat inside the area a little longer to wash the boat out and trying to get in a good place to try to get the boat turned around and facing back out.

Kent noticed the bilge pumps were working a lot. Kent looked at the crew and said, "We have to figure out why the bilge pumps are coming on." And he needed to see why, if the plugs had come out, so the boat would require the pump to come on.

After the crew lifted the hatch, he noticed all the plugs were in place and said, "There is no reason why it should be pumping as much as it is."

Kent looked at him and said, "I think I do. We took that run offshore, and I think with the rough weather and the way it was coming out of the water, I think we split the bottom of the boat." Now before heading in and shutting the engine off and listening to make sure there were no other boats in the area so they could make sure they did not give away their location as to where they hid the stash at, they fired the boat back up and pushed back through the green door, easing along and not trying to make too much noise, when Kent and the crew were talking about the other crews, wondering if they made it or sunk or whatever happened to them. The big worry was you never knew what was waiting for you when you hit the docks.

The bilge pumps were still pumping. Kent knew he could not leave the boat in the water. She would sink before daylight. On the south side of the island, there was a spot that had tapered land, and Kent ran the boat to that side of the island, and after being two hundred feet off the bank, he hit the gas and ran the boat high and dry on beach it to keep it out of the water.

Now everyone was starting to return and getting back in. The clan would gather to make sure everyone was all right. Kent would have a new boat before morning because they had them already waiting for them with new motors, and new boats would be ready to go.

The next morning, everybody was meeting at the Oyster Bar Tavern. Talking over what had happened the night before when Kent learned that his crewmen dove overboard and swam in. When they went back to look for him, there was no sign of him on the island, with no scratches or bug bites on him, and this was where the Daniels clan learned that this crewman was just like his brother who came out of prison and turned out to be the government informant.

CHAPTER THIRTY-SEVEN

End to an Era

After an eighteen-month investigation, Operation Everglades Two came down, and the Daniels crew was at the top of the list to be arrested, along with anyone else that was not included in Operation Everglades One.

Isn't it ironic that the Daniels family and several other organizations who had crews were prosecuted and incarcerated for being accused of hauling marijuana into our country and working for our government and never being caught with anything in their possession and giving up approximately seventy-five years of their lives away from their families and friends to now see marijuana is starting to be legalized across the United States.

Isn't it ironic, and it makes you wonder if they weren't used as an example, and the legalization was coming anyway.

When the Daniels family found out that the indictment was coming down, they hauled the marijuana right up until they contacted their attorney, and they asked the government not to come in kicking the doors down, but the government wouldn't hear of it. They had to have the publicity. They raided the town, kicking in doors and shooting dogs that were in the front yard, babies crying, wives being pulled out of bed.

They now proceeded to the Daniels homes, and no one was there. At this time, the cop standing there started laughing, and the other agent asked what was so funny, and the laughing agent said to the other, "They are true to their form."

The cops looked at him and said, "What?"

"This is why they were called the ghost people. We never could catch them with anything. Now you see them, and now you don't. They eluded us again."

The local law enforcement that ran the families off their land was bought off by the crews to run the marijuana through and into the Ten Thousand Islands. The trail of the money went deep into law enforcement up to their upper management and beyond. Certain people of the other crews that were favored by the local law enforcement more than the others allowed special privileges to be given to them inside the national park, with fishing as well as hauling marijuana.

Even when they were transported from to the area to Miami, the law enforcement had enough respect to protect them from the media coverage that normally came out during these transports. The crew was taken from Naples, where they turned themselves in and then transported to Miami.

The judge heard the case and the bail was set; the family paid it, and they were released to speak to their attorneys when an agreement had been reached with the government that the crew could never be charged with anything else if they agreed to the conditions. Randal and Darryl were hit the hardest, with both being charged with racketeering, and they were named the kingpin, making them carry the toughest and the longest sentences of all the group.

As with anything, all good things must come to an end. With the new laws that came down under our new president making the consequences much more severe than ever before, the men involved in this new industry were now facing one hundred years to life in prison if they were caught, which made this a game-changer.

Life as they knew it was gone, and the last frontier emerged again, but with stricter limitations on the commercial fishing industry, which was the primary way of life to earn a living in this area. With a slower pace in life and with limited ways to survive, the poverty set back in.

The little sleepy fishing village was once again removed from the hustle and the bustle of the fast-paced life, with the flashy cars, airplanes, new boats, and all the jewelry that sparkled in the sunlight. Now reality set in one more time.

With time and age, the Daniels clan gave up marijuana smuggling, and the daring life subsided, and the famous Ghost People of the Everglades mellowed, as we all do. They contacted their attorney and made a deal with the United States government to turn themselves in. The Daniels clan stood trial and served approximately seventy-five years in total altogether.

Let's be clear on one thing, the Daniels clan was never caught with any drugs. All their charges were conspiracy- and racketeering-related. All time had been completed and served. Some of the clan have remained in the area, struggling with the day-to-day hostile life that came with the territory of living in the Everglades. Others had gone on to be with the Lord and are dearly missed every day.

ABOUT THE AUTHOR

 Barbara Tyner Hall is a mother of three wonderful grown kids and a true entrepreneur at heart who is eager to show her passion for writing about all sorts of stories that she has encountered through her travels, hard work, and imagination. She has a unique talent and style that can place you in the story through her compelling and descriptive writing without leaving your home. Barbara divides her time between her two favorite states, Texas and Florida, where she writes full time.

CPSIA information can be obtained
at www.ICGtesting.com
Printed in the USA
LVHW111939260121
677442LV00025B/1063